# BREAKING FATE

## BOOK THREE: BLACK CLAW RANCH

### CECILIA LANE

A SHIFTING DESTINIES NOVEL

Breaking Fate: Black Claw Ranch #3 by Cecilia Lane
March 2019

# CONTENTS

# CHAPTER 1

Sloan Kent stared at the man across the table. Daryl Jones, aged forty-six, held for questioning on a long list of crimes, chewed slowly and deliberately. She was damn sure if she cared enough to count, he chewed each mouthful of fast-food burger one hundred times between bites.

She'd seen the tactic before, and she didn't let it phase her in the slightest. He could take his sweet time. She had nowhere else to be. That was the down and upside of not being fully trusted by her new unit. She wasn't given much to do, but she had time to babysit a perp in interrogation.

Daryl was one of a handful still in the holding cells of the new Supernatural Enforcement Agency field office situated right outside Bearden, Montana.

They'd picked the asshole up during a raid on a hunter cell, where he'd happily discharged his weapon into the body armor of agents attempting to take down his boss. The big man shouted 'lawyer' as soon as the cuffs were around his wrists, but the grunts guarding him weren't so lucky to have legal counsel on retainer.

Daryl slurped at his soda and wiped his mouth with the back of his hand, ignoring the napkin next to the wrapper. "You're not one of them."

Sloan leaned back in her chair. "I'm an agent."

"That ain't what I mean. One of *them*. You're human." He waved a finger in front of his eyes. "Yours haven't changed color once. Not like those freaks."

Only human on the shifter squad, in fact. Smart that he'd picked up on it. Though with his allegiance so proudly declared for the human side, she shouldn't have been surprised.

"You're right." She placed her hands on the table and pitched forward. "So you know how it feels to be the odd man out."

His flashed smile didn't reach his eyes. "What can you expect from these fucks? They're unnatural."

"Abominations, your boss called them. You can't even tell what they are by looking at them. Could be a bear in their middle, or even a badger." That one had come as a shock to many. The woman in question had recently moved to Bearden and got caught up in some sort of revenge plot to sell her to the hunter group. One of her abductors was a shifter herself, proving all manner of assholes existed across species. "And we don't know how many exist, or how they got here in the first place."

The tactic was meant to form a bond, the words lifted from interviews with others picked up in the same raid. If Sloan could get Daryl talking, maybe he'd slip up with more information for the investigation. He was just one small piece in a bigger machine the SEA claimed it wanted to dismantle.

The wheels of justice turned slowly when the people at the top didn't actually want change.

Daryl relaxed slightly. "Would these bleeding hearts be so accepting if they was aliens come to butt-probe their sons and daughters?"

"They just don't understand, do they? Not like you and your friends. You guys have your ideals. Standing up for something, I can respect that."

He grunted.

"Bet you know all sorts of places to go and ways to find like-minded individuals." Not taking her eyes off him, she clicked her pen and held it over a pad of paper. "So I'm asking, what were you planning on doing with the two you had locked up?"

The light attitude he'd beamed at her disappeared.

"You think I don't know you?" Daryl asked darkly.

Sloan clicked the pen closed and set it down with a measured sigh of annoyance. "Well, I don't know you."

"You're that cunt bitch who sent away Culpepper."

Fuck.

The name sent a shudder of disgust down her spine, followed by a sickening unease.

How many eyes watched from behind the glass? How many would spout off that bit of knowledge the moment they reached another friendly ear?

How many already knew, and reported her every move back to Jimmy and his friends?

"It's Snitch Bitch, actually, and he's not your concern." Sloan didn't even blink. The words rolled right off her back and even if they struck a nerve, she wasn't about to let Daryl the Scumbag see it. "You're looking at charges for assaulting a federal agent, illegal possession of a firearm, trafficking, and hate crimes. You're in a world of trouble,

Daryl. Only way to stop it crushing you is to start talking."

"Only human here. Only one willing to work with those fucking freaks out there. You always been a traitor, or is it just because you got some animal kinks in your closet?" He held up two fingers and wagged his tongue in the space between. "Let me loose, and I'll fuck you back to the right side of things."

He wanted to get a rise out of her. She grew up around cops and tough boys who thought their worth was measured by the size of their dicks. Daryl Jones was on the inchworm side of the scale. "Think long and hard about the next words to come out of your mouth," she said evenly, "and whether your boss will have the same loyalty to you when he's cutting deals with that fancy lawyer of his."

"I'm not making deals with a snitch bitch!"

Snitch Bitch. She wore the name like armor. She'd be damned before she let Jimmy Culpepper and his friends know how much their actions and harassment continued to sting.

Sloan could see how a man passed over for promotion, with two kids in private school and an ex-wife demanding more alimony could boil over when a perp took a swing at him. She understood that, had a frame of reference for it in her head. She didn't support it by any means, and did her fucking best to defuse any situation that turned too hot.

What Jimmy did? That wasn't getting rough with a suspect. That was torture. She'd nearly lost the contents of her stomach when she rode up on the scene.

So yeah, she reported him. She went into gruesome detail to make sure the incident wasn't swept under the rug. No one deserved the treatment she saw. Justice was blind for a reason and everyone—human, shifter, and even the probe-happy aliens—deserved their slice of it.

Her reward? Transfer papers to the newly formed shifter division within the SEA.

Girl cop, girl fed. Snitch Bitch. Human on the shifter squad. She didn't have a place of her own. She was the round puzzle piece trying to fit in a world of square pegs. Sloan tried not to let being on the outside bother her. She'd grown tough over the years because of it. A little thing like not being trusted with more than filing the paperwork or talking to suspects wouldn't break her.

Even the last wasn't entirely her own. She knew eyes observed from behind the glass. Daryl-fucking-

Jones might as well have made an announcement over the intercom.

Sloan wanted to throttle the man.

Daryl crossed his arms over his chest and leveled her with a blank gaze. "Lawyer."

She shrugged, keeping her face blank. There went a chance to prove her worth and end her sidelining. She couldn't even get one of the hunters talking; why the hell would her new boss give her anything of value to do? "If that's the way you want to play it. This is all out of my hands now. I can't help you if you call in some slime ball."

"Lawyer," he repeated.

Sloan opened her mouth to try reasoning with him again, but a knock on the glass cut her short.

"Time's up," she said as she pushed to her feet. "You really should have talked."

Sloan stepped out of the box to find Mara Vaughn and Desmond Crewe staring at each other like two bushy-tailed cats.

"I don't care what good you thought you were doing," Crewe hissed. "You're here only to consult. You don't get to make decisions on who gets released, and when."

Not wanting to interrupt anything she didn't

need to hear, Sloan brushed aside and made her way to her desk.

She had a fair idea of what brought on the dressing down. Mara served as a consultant for the SEA on all matters related to hunters. She didn't have a badge and wasn't allowed out in the field. While everyone else geared up and rolled out, she'd been left alone with a clan of civilians that'd been picked up while searching for one of their own. Instead of keeping them contained while the agents raided the hunter meeting, Mara set them free.

One face flashed to the front of her mind, and Sloan quickly shoved it away. She didn't have time for dark-eyed men who'd just get intimidated by her service weapon. And she certainly didn't want to tangle with a beefy cowboy who wouldn't listen to officers of the law.

Crewe, the agent in charge of the entire field office, had his work cut out for him in making the squad into a proper team even without consultants going rogue. He had some recruits from his military days, as well as any of the shifters who'd snuck their way into the SEA before they were technically allowed in the ranks. Instead of firing them outright and facing possible legal challenges, the bosses just shuffled them into the Bearden office.

Outcasts and misfits and snitch bitches, oh my.

Muted conversations died as she entered the bullpen.

Sloan tried to let that roll off her back, just like Daryl's words in the interrogation room. It was a bit more difficult when she knew every single one of the sidelong glancers could smell her emotions.

Fuck. If they didn't trust her before, they sure as shit wouldn't trust her now. She was supposed to have her partner's back, not put him behind bars.

She said a silent curse to the sleaze who outed her.

This wasn't how she imagined her career would go. She knew it wouldn't be sunshine and rainbows, but feeling as scummy as the assholes she tried to put away? She'd done what anyone in their right mind would do, but she was still eyed with suspicion.

And that was discounting all the threats and hissed words from Jimmy's closest friends. Sloan moved out of their immediate reach when she received her transfer papers, but they were persistent in making her pay.

Snitch Bitch. Human on the shifter squad. Living in Bearden made her feel more alone than ever.

With a growl that rivaled any of her shifter

coworkers, Sloan tumbled into her seat and snatched up the pile of mail that'd been dropped off while she was in the box with Daryl. Desk duty. She had years under her belt as a beat cop, then more as a federal agent before requesting a transfer into the SEA, and she'd been relegated to fucking mail sorting and report filing.

She wouldn't break. Jimmy's people slashing her tires and leaving notes in her locker hadn't intimidated her to change her story. She wouldn't give up making a place for herself in her new field office. The world needed good police, and she intended to fight for the side of justice until she drew her last breath.

Her father's memory deserved nothing less. The old man placed as high a value on serving his fellow man as she did. She'd learned from the best.

She tried to imagine what he'd say to her if he were still alive. Something profound like *hold the course*, or *fuck those pricks*.

She chose both. Fuck 'em. She was there to stay.

Sloan slid a finger under the sealed edge of the padded envelope and ripped it open.

"What the fuck?"

All eyes whipped to her, then down to the mess in her lap. Silence fell over the room, punctuated by the gurgling of the coffee machine from the break room.

Sloan stared at the crumbled snake skins decorating her slacks.

Because she was a snake who sent her partner away. Clever.

She couldn't roll her eyes hard enough.

The pause of shock went on just a second too long. Her coworkers waited for someone else to step in first, to take the hit in seeming like they cared.

Mara was the one that saved them from pretending. "You sure pissed someone off," she said.

Her words broke the spell over the rest and they turned back to whatever tasks and conversations she'd interrupted.

"My specialty," Sloan muttered.

"You and me both." Mara grabbed up a trash can and plopped it down at her feet.

Sloan brushed the dried and breaking skins into the garbage and tried not to imagine she was doing the same to her career.

"Briefing room. Now," Crewe ordered as he swept past.

Sloan cleared her throat as she pushed to her feet. "Thanks for that."

"Don't mention it. I've been in your shoes." Mara

shrugged. "Give them time to get used to you. And if they don't, break their balls until they're forced to respect you."

Sloan barked a laugh. A thin bit of strain faded from her shoulders with her first pleasant interaction in the office. Maybe she was finally reaching a turning point.

The Jimmy Culpeppers and Daryl Joneses of the world would need to work a lot harder to spook her into giving up her sense of right and wrong.

She just needed to figure out a way to survive everything else.

## CHAPTER 2

Lorne Bennett heeled his horse ahead of the others. Streaks of purple and orange colored the sky overhead as the last bit of daylight dwindled into nothing. One more hill, then they'd be home. Just a little further until he could shed the annoyances of the clan and find solace in being alone.

His bones and bear ached with the need for... something. Solitude, definitely. A shift, likely. That could be done without the others squawking behind him.

He was tempted to gallop ahead and skip the big dinner, but then it wouldn't be just the men of his clan shooting him questioning looks. He didn't want to disappoint the mates. Tansey would probably kill him and grind him up for the next meal, but Joss would make her eyes wide and smell sad. She'd been through enough without him sullying the celebration of a new mate bond.

"We'll need to move the herd tomorrow," Ethan, his alpha, said. "I want a proper count on the calves, too. None of the guesstimating bullshit you've been giving me the last few times."

"Yeah, Jesse," Hunter interjected with the snap of a preteen.

"I was talking to you, asshole," Ethan growled back. "Do you even know how to count, or are you just lazy?"

"Of course I can count. I counted getting Joss off six times last night—"

Everyone behind him groaned. Lorne just shot a glare over his shoulder and hunched further in on himself.

His bear paced in his head. Talk of mates did that lately. His skin had felt itchy and too tight the moment Tansey and Ethan paired up and only worsened when Hunter set his eyes on Joss.

He tried to keep his distance while they established new families. And it wasn't just his clan. Seemed everyone in Bearden was finding their perfect match. Going into town for food or supplies was heading straight into a bright, shiny world where everyone had the sort of love that stuck to their ribs and made them fat with happiness.

His bear slashed his inside hard enough to make Lorne clench his fists.

He didn't have a mate. Couldn't. He refused to put a woman in mourning black and have her cry over him when he was gone. His fate was death, and there was no breaking away from that final ending.

A tough face framed by blonde hair pushed through his antsy bear's growls. Bright blue eyes that reminded him of the Montana skies pierced his tattered soul.

His bear quieted with the memory of the SEA agent they'd briefly glimpsed while in lockup. Her face had haunted him all through the night and day. He'd tossed the shirt he'd been wearing into his laundry basket before digging it out and huffing it for any trace of her scent.

He hadn't even caught her name.

His bear slumped down and let off a mournful howl.

Not his concern. If he ran into her again, maybe he'd flash her a smile and try to get her alone for a night. There was no use looking for anything more than temporary when he could die at any moment.

The Black Claw barn appeared in the distance and a tiny fraction of relief surged inside Lorne. Soon. He just had to stay steady for a little while longer, then he could shake the others for the night.

Lorne sped through stabling his mare, ignoring the insults and smacks the others lobbed in every direction. Nova flicked her brown ears in his direction and pawed at the fresh hay with her one white foot. Lorne suppressed a smile. He knew what she wanted. He paused to give her a scratch behind her ears and an extra handful of oats. She was a good lady, and entirely undeserving of the tension riding roughshod over him.

He steeled himself to step out of the stall and was immediately hit by a carrot sailing through the air.

Lorne stared down at the vegetable projectile and shook his head. "Idiots," he muttered.

Hunter's face split into a grin and he raised a fist in the air. "Truth speaker!"

Truth speaker. He doubted any of them knew how deep the words cut him. They used it because he only spoke when he had something to say; he'd earned it when he called out his family on being horrible assholes who placed too much value on their persecution complexes.

Not that they knew the details. He kept them at a distance the same as anyone else. He didn't want to be missed when he was gone.

His bear rolled through him again. The beast craved companionship and hated their solitary life. The beast wanted him to brush up against Hunter, throw an arm around Ethan's shoulders, even give a manly punch of affection to Jesse. Staying out of step with the bears he was clanned up and pledged to rubbed him raw and made him want to fight.

A flick of his eyes and a test of the air gauged the others around him. Alex was always down for a brawl. Hunter, too, but then he was still riding the high of a brand new mate mark. That exuberance had annoyed the piss out of each and every one of the others, even more than his usual cavalier attitude. Jesse glowered in Hunter's general direction, the even keel he tried to maintain tipping off balance.

"Truth speaking would be asking what tricks you played on that poor woman up at the house." Lorne scratched at his beard. Damn thing itched hideously. He'd intended to shave it off that morning, but his bear kept his skin until the very last possible moment. Too many shifts, too long in his other shape. Irritation poisoned him from the inside out. He needed the fight.

Ethan shot him a look. Yeah, his alpha knew what he was doing. The silence allowed it to happen anyway.

"We already know Tansey's batshit insane for locking down this asshole," Alex jumped in and jerked his thumb in Ethan's direction. "What's Joss's excuse?"

Hunter growled. "There's nothing wrong with her. She's the most perfect woman in the entire world.

"But she wants to stare at your ugly face for the rest of her life?" Alex insisted. "That's where I get lost."

Lorne grunted his support.

"Just because ladies constantly confuse your two ends doesn't mean we're all cursed in that department." Hunter smacked his lips in an offensive kiss. "Just ask your mother."

"You motherfucker," Alex snarled.

"Well, not anymore," Hunter laughed. He buffed his fingernails against his shirt. "I'm a happily mated man now."

A growl sawed out of Alex as he threw his fist into Hunter's stomach.

Fuck *yes*.

Hunter slammed a blow back into Alex and sent him stumbling into Jesse. The clan's second pushed him off with a growl of his own.

Feeling the fight building on all sides, Alex's bear ripped out of him and roared.

Ethan simply shook his head and ran a hand down his face.

Hunter shifted, blond bear stepping up to the challenge. Jesse, too, joined in for the fight.

His own inner animal pacing away, Lorne let the bear take his skin.

His aching bones popped with relief as they broke apart and reformed. Muscles tore and clenched and grew back stronger than before.

Anger and frustration flowed out of him with every swipe of his paws. Each blow that connected cut away the ropes tightly binding him into obedience. Relief flooded him with the stretched muscles and rising scent of drawn blood. He was a hulking murder machine, and anything less was unacceptable.

He clipped Hunter's legs and sent him tumbling ass over ears. Jesse latched onto his side and sank his fangs deep, but Lorne just shook him off. He rose up on hind feet and swung a heavy paw at Alex's face.

Alex roared in fury.

Lorne felt that frenzy in his bones. Alex's anger was like a flash fire, sparking up over nothing and flaming out just as fast. His own was just as mighty, but it burned slow. He'd had years to stoke the flames and let the blaze consume him.

Every blow he dealt was another for Lilah.

Each snap of his jaws fought off a brother, a cousin, someone he called a friend.

They turned a quiet, thoughtful boy into a killer.

The four of them tumbled out of the barn and into the yard between buildings. He was vaguely aware of Tansey and Joss standing on the porch, one with her arms crossed with silent reproach and the other clasping her hands together under her chin in a picture of worry.

Lorne turned into the bear barreling toward him with renewed strength. He'd never have a mate to guard his back or to give him an earful for acting like a fool. His family had stolen that from him, too, and his new clan were the ones to pay.

The beast of a bear slapped him with deadly claws, drawing blood from the side of his face. Lorne sank into those wounds and dealt his own with a roar.

They crashed through the paddock fence and a sharp whistle cracked through the air.

"Enough!" Ethan yelled.

A cold spray of water hit him square in the chest before turning to blast Alex in the face.

The soft sound of women's laughter broke through the anger clouding up his head. He shook his body and sent water droplets flying in all directions, only to have the hose turned on him again.

"I've been waiting ages for the chance to do that!" Tansey yelled at them.

"You're a monster," Ethan hollered back.

All around, shapes shimmered from bear back to human. For most, the brawl simply faded away into the countless number of however many they'd fought over the years. Not for him. Lorne still itched with the need to set his world right, and the frustration of it never happening made him want to bite and snarl all over again.

Joss screeched as Hunter wrapped his arms around her waist and chased the spray of the hose to get her wet. He slipped in the mud and they both went down in a tangle of limbs and laughter.

Lorne heaved in a fresh breath and tried to smile.

Exhaustion weighed down his lips. The clan was a mess, and he didn't belong.

His problems didn't matter. He wouldn't put them on anyone else, nor would he ruin the party.

He swiveled his head to the redhead covered in mud splatters and shrugged. "Welcome to the clan, Joss."

# CHAPTER 3

E than had barely pulled off the bumpy, single track road leading away from Black Claw when he cleared his throat. "So."

Lorne pulled his Stetson down over his eyes and considered throwing himself from the truck. They weren't going too fast. He'd survived worse than road rash.

He should have guessed there was more to the trip than a simple supply run. Oh, they were low on feed and needed fence posts and wire and other things to make the ranch run smoothly, but he didn't count on the talking beforehand. Ethan had him pinned down with no chance of escape.

Lorne eyed the road zipping past with renewed interest.

"You've been fighting more than usual," Ethan continued.

He grunted. No sense in denying a fact they both knew.

"Coming up on the time you joined us, isn't it?"

His way of asking if Lorne needed extra watching.

Anniversaries didn't make a lick of difference to him. He wasn't Alex, who, like clockwork, went more nuts than usual around the same time every year.

But he'd been fighting more, just as Ethan said. Or rather, prodding the others into it to give him the excuse.

Tansey's arrival kicked a hornet's nest inside him. His brain buzzed with the need for more than the quiet, unassuming life he'd cut out for himself on Black Claw.

Lorne locked down his bear before the beast could echo the desire or push sendings of that SEA agent his way. Blonde hair tucked up and ready to be ruined, blue eyes he wanted to see darken, curves hidden away under all those layers like presents to be unwrapped.

Fuck, too late. Those visions were of his ideal

woman. Her remembered scent drove him just as crazy, too. Sweet and delicious and not his.

"Tansey didn't say anything, did she? You know she pops off without thinking."

Lorne snorted. "I think she knows exactly what comes out of her mouth."

Ethan frowned slightly, like he'd been given a truth that he didn't know how to handle. Then he shook himself and tried again. "That shit yesterday—"

"Made sure we got through the party without anyone shifting or storming off. Got the whole thing started with a mud fight—"

"Broke our damn paddock fence," Ethan muttered darkly.

Lorne shrugged. "I'm fine."

"You're not." Ethan tapped his temple. "You assholes give me a constant headache. We have another round of guests coming in the next week, and trail rides booked all summer. I need to know if someone in my clan is unsteady."

"Yeah, well, you don't have to worry about me. Steady as she goes."

"Lie."

Lorne glared at him darkly and jammed his hat back over his face.

CECILIA LANE

At least Ethan took the hint and didn't prod him again. Or order him to talk, like some power-mad alpha. The silence hung heavily between them for the rest of the ride into town.

He usually liked the trip. He didn't spend much time off the ranch, except to head to the local bars. Supply runs meant pit stops followed with a lunch at either the diner or the barbecue joint before heading back to the dirt and cows.

Agitation huddled in his chest instead. He just wanted to get what was needed and get back to the ranch. He didn't want small talk or more probing into his shit attitude or the reasons why he was on edge. Fuck, he'd give just about anything for a brawl at that exact moment.

Maybe he needed to sever every connection to the place and get the hell out of Bearden.

The thought of leaving made his stomach feel hollow. So there he was, stuck. One foot in the grave, one walking slow circles around the rim, and neither quieting any of the unwanted static in his mind.

Dark clouds hanging over his head, he followed Ethan into the feed store.

They were three aisles and a load of supplies deep when the first sour scent twitched his nose. Unbelieving, he inhaled again.

26

Lorne stiffened. His bear stood straight up in the back of his mind, ears flicking on high alert.

The scent that invaded his nose was imprinted on his mind. Soft and earthy, just like his own. Under it was something darker and more prickly. Something deadly. That scent brought back memories of blood and screaming. He could feel a noose tightening around his neck with every inhale.

Ian.

Fuck.

Lorne shot glances in every direction and tried to spot the man. His eyes bounced over him twice before he settled a glare in his direction.

Ian stood tall right near the doors, his dark hair clipped shorter than Lorne remembered. The growth spurt that had just started the last time he laid eyes on his cousin had produced a solid man packed with muscle. He expected nothing less. Bennetts were raised to be weapons in a war that had never arrived.

*Fuck.*

He'd been a dead man walking for years that felt like centuries. He'd avoided his execution once. Now the family had found him and would finish the job.

His bear boiled up to the surface. Lorne tried to kick the beast to the back of his head, but the creature wouldn't budge. A throbbing headache pulsed right behind his eyes and his gums ached with the press of fangs. Flashed images sped through his mind of past threats and present dangers.

Ian could try, but the bear wouldn't go down without a fight.

Useless. Stupid animal. Their fate was decided ages ago and he'd postponed it for too long.

Lorne switched directions and made a beeline back to Ethan.

"I need to leave," he said gruffly.

Needed to get away from witnesses. Needed to lessen the collateral damage.

"No fucking chance," Ethan scoffed absently. "We still have more stops to make. Lumber ain't going to buy itself."

"Ethan."

His tone broke through whatever thoughts floated through his alpha's head. Blue eyes found his without a hint of reproach.

"They found me."

Ethan's eyebrows tried to meld with his hairline. "You're certain?"

"Scented and spotted. Not someone I'm likely to forget."

How could he? They'd taken something beautiful and turned it ugly. He'd been so young and aged a lifetime in just a few short moments. Bastards, the whole rotten lot of them.

"They going to be a problem?"

Concern washed through Ethan's scent as he fixed silver eyes on Lorne. He knew the crazy bears under him were down for a fight. But mates were involved now. Tansey would probably love to wade right in, and Joss could hold her own if pushed. Ethan and Hunter would rather lose a limb than see either woman anywhere near a real battle.

He should have left the moment Ethan set his eyes on Tansey. The writing had been on the wall. His place wasn't on a ranch with happily paired up couples.

"No," Lorne said with a shake of his head. "I won't let them become one."

Ethan rubbed the back of his neck and rolled his eyes to the ceiling. "The old homestead on the far edge of the ranch could use some fixing up, I suppose. Last time we passed by, looked like the lions were using it as a scratching post. You should probably grab some grub and head out that way."

He dug the truck keys out of his pocket and

handed them over. "Get gone. I'll call up to the house and have Tansey come back this way when you drop off the truck."

No other questions, no chiding about the extra time added to a necessary chore. Ethan was a good alpha. Tansey had made him a great man.

"Lorne?"

He stopped in his tracks with a grunt, but didn't turn around. He didn't want to see any pity or whatever other bullshit sad face Ethan was making.

"You tag us in if you need to. You're one of us. We fight for our people."

*Our people.* Lorne turned the words over and over as he made his way out to the parking lot. He wasn't anyone's people. His own people tried to kill him.

He needed to clear out of Bearden entirely, not just to the edge of Black Claw territory. He was just having trouble putting his feet into motion. Better to draw the danger away before it spilled over on Ethan's people.

A new scent stopped him in his tracks and nearly brought him to his knees.

*Her.*

Soft and sweet, like strawberries and cream. Something layered under it, not unlike oil for servicing a weapon.

Lorne glanced across the parking lot. Thirty, maybe forty feet away, she leaned against the side of a black SUV marked with Supernatural Enforcement Agency insignia.

His bear roared at him to close the distance. His heart seized against his ribcage and his legs locked him in place.

She looked even more lovely in the light of day. Her hair was pinned back in a professional style that made him want to yank it all out and let it flow between his fingers. He wasn't a stranger to run-ins with the law, and he could spot when a rookie wasn't comfortable with the power they wielded. Not her. She looked like a fucking queen.

Lorne glanced over his shoulder. No sign of Ian, but he had to be near.

With a growl, he wrenched himself free of his bear's cement-like grip over his body. Another time, place, life, and he'd have sauntered over and dipped the brim of his hat. He wanted to hear her voice and feel her lips curve against his.

He wanted to punch fate in the dick. Whatever her name, however she held his bear's attention, he couldn't get close. To her, or to anyone. He wouldn't put anyone else in the line of danger. His family, his problem.

He was a dead man. Running only postponed the inevitable.

He wouldn't drag her down with him.

# CHAPTER 4

Sloan glared at the dark clouds rolling her way. She cocked her head and listened for the muffled roar of an ATV, but she didn't have shifter senses and the last of the sound had faded almost an hour ago when her partner, August Snow, suggested they split up and take separate routes while patrolling the edge of enclave territory.

She was being hazed, and she knew it. Newbies on the team were always treated to something. Prank calls from Seymour Butts or messages to call back Mr. Lion at the local zoo were innocent compared to being shoved onto patrol and abandoned. She should have known something was up from the very start. She'd gone weeks without any significant work, and now they wanted her out on patrol? Only thing to do was grin and bear it.

Hah. Bear it. Bearden. Bears all around.

Her GPS chirped at her, but the signal didn't give her anything of use. The tiny dot that indicated her position bounced back and forth over the area. She bet her partner knew that, too, and didn't mention it on purpose.

Grumbling to herself, Sloan sank back into her seat and urged the ATV forward. Best to get on with finding her way back to the office. Good lord, she wanted to figure it out and shove it in their faces. She might be human, but she wasn't incapable.

She eyed the mountains behind her. Bearden was that direction, she knew. The land ahead of her would take her back to the field office. But where exactly, what angle she needed to take, she had little idea. She wasn't a tracker. She'd grown up and worked in cities all her life. Without street signs or skyscraper landmarks, she relied purely on guesswork.

Fucking hazing.

At least the scenery was a nice change from big buildings and noisy traffic. More peaceful, too. Hills rolled in every direction, thick with summer growth of grass and wildflowers where they hadn't been chomped down by hungry cattle. The mountains were sharp and jagged and eerily beautiful. Even the looming dark clouds clashing against the bright blue of the summer day were a sight to behold.

She turned the ATV back toward the field office. Or at least, what she hoped would be close enough for her to find her way. She wasn't ready to give up and radio in for directions. They wanted to wave their dicks around and put her in her place, fine. She'd prove her worth.

Sloan resigned herself to a thorough soaking when the first fat raindrop landed on her arm and she was no closer to finding shelter. Even pushing the ATV to its maximum speed didn't outrun the storm. Wisps of hair soon clung to her face and neck, her shirt and pants were soaked, and the wind cut right through to chill her skin.

She slowed as she neared a house she definitely hadn't passed before. She'd ridden too far, then. Shit.

But... Sloan chewed her lip. There was a roof, even if it tilted a little too far to one side. Four walls, though they looked marred by long gouges in the wood. The rundown house was better than staying out in the rain. She could wait it out. Summer storms never lasted long.

She zipped closer and stopped when she found

the fence peeled back. A tangle of barbed wire curled near some fence posts like the work had been abandoned. Caught on a spike was a tuft of fur. Large paw prints marred the earth on both sides of the fence.

Sloan hesitated. Shifters were territorial. They clumped up like animals in the wild and didn't take kindly to surprises. Her uniform, too, wasn't a welcome sight by many because of dirty cops like Jimmy. She wanted to do her part to fix that image, but making a stand in the middle of nowhere wasn't the place to do it.

A shiver ran down her spine. Sloan couldn't shake the feeling of being watched and hunted. By those with animals under their skins, or her former partner and the rest of his sick little cabal, she didn't know. Stupid, but it fueled the growing pit in her stomach.

Then the storm broke with a vengeance and so did her patience.

"Motherfuckers!" she yelled at the unseen watchers.

She could imagine how the conversation went down in the break room. So funny, stranding the human out on the range. Hilarious, to do it with a storm brewing. Let's see how soon she cries for mercy and leaves for a unit filled with her own kind.

Too bad for them. She wasn't one to give up easily. "I'm not running away! There's nowhere else for me to go, so get used to me! Assholes!"

Movement near the house caught her eye and she whipped her head to the side. The wind picked up at that moment, taking the man's hat right off his head. It tumbled past her, end over end, into the distance.

He charged at her, waving his arms and shouting incomprehensible words. Sloan cut the engine and dropped her hand to her service weapon. He didn't miss a single step.

She'd seen him before, briefly. Those dark eyes bored into her with the same intensity a few nights ago. And that hair? Looked even sexier when wet and plastered against his head.

He tore through the hole in the fence and tugged her off the ATV. "What the hell are you doing out here in the middle of all this?" he growled.

Sloan struggled, but there was no pulling away from him. Digging in her feet only resulted in him dragging her a few steps until she stumbled back to a walk.

Dread filled her. Shifter, of course. And she was overpowered within seconds. She'd never doubted her ability to take care of herself until that moment. Close calls, run-ins with suspects, she'd fought hard and knew she stood a chance. The dark-haired cowboy ruined that notion in an instant.

She hated how her skin seemed to bloom with warmth where his hand connected.

He rounded the ramshackle home and started toward a dark opening at the side.

She finally yanked herself free of his grasp. "I'm not going down there."

"Then have fun dealing with the tornado that got spotted a couple miles from here." He jerked his chin down the dark stairs. "In."

Sloan wrestled with the idea of never seeing the light of day again after being locked in some cowboy's murder shack and the fine hairs lifting all over her body. She wanted to trust the man still peering at her with eyes hot enough to set her on fire.

She took a cautious first step, followed by another. Her eyes adjusted slowly to the low light. The cellar was cool and, most importantly, dry.

She did *not* jump when the doors to the outside slammed shut.

Air buffeted her as the cowboy swept past. He

clicked something, then a lantern filled the space with soft light and shadows.

"You said something about a tornado?"

He grunted and rummaged through a bag on the ground.

"Aren't there supposed to be alarms or something to warn people?"

"We're not living in a movie, sweetheart." A flicker of a smile graced his lips. "The mountains usually break up the worst storms. Tornados aren't common enough around here to call for any sirens."

Good to know. She stashed the information away to turn over at another time.

He tossed her a bundle that turned out to be a towel, an oversized shirt, and sweatpants. "You should change out of those wet clothes. Don't you humans catch cold from a little water, or something?"

Sloan narrowed her eyes, but her retort died on her lips.

Oh, holy hell. He whipped off his shirt to reveal an expanse of muscles underneath. His hips even had those carved lines that made smart girls go stupid over a man. Sloan worked to swallow because she wasn't immune to them in the slightest.

The hot cowboy was even hotter than she imagined. She wanted to lick a line down each of those indentations, straight to whatever he was hiding underneath.

She spun around when his hands went to his jeans. "Is there anywhere else you could do that?"

His huffed a laugh. "Look around, sweetheart. Does this cellar look like a mansion?"

Clothes rustled behind her, then dropped in a thick, wet splat on the floor. Her eyes bounced from one corner of the wall in front of her to the other. She would not turn around. She would not peek over her shoulder. Perving out on the man was inappropriate. She mentally smacked her hands in admonishment. "Is this your place?"

"You always ask this many questions?"

Sloan wrapped the towel around her shoulders. She wouldn't change out of uniform in front of him, but she was grateful for the extra layer and to wipe her face and arms. "Nature of the job. You always this elusive?"

"Nature of the job. You can turn around now."

He'd pulled on a fresh pair of jeans and shirt. They stretched nicely over his ass and back as he bent to shake out and drape his wet clothes over a plastic basin sink.

She shook the dirty thoughts out of her head as a

shiver worked down her spine. The cooler air and soaked clothes, she told herself. "And what job is that, exactly?"

He touched his finger to an imaginary hat. "Cattle rancher. Occasional tour guide. Currently, hospitality manager for the You're Welcome Corral."

"I'll pass on these." She tossed the shirt and sweats into the bag on the floor. "Thanks for the towel."

Quiet stretched between them as his eyes roved down her body. Heat spread through her limbs under his gaze. The air around him seemed almost alive with electricity when he returned gold eyes to her face.

Wild. He had a wild animal under his skin. She couldn't forget that he was part man, part animal, and potentially dangerous as both.

No, not dangerous. At least, not in the physical harm sense of the word. Something about him made her immediately reject the idea. Gut instinct. Maybe something in his eyes, unnatural as they were.

But a dangerous temptation? Yeah, he had her attention.

"My alpha's folks bought the land with this already on it," he explained quietly. The answer to her previous question felt like a concession, like he'd judged her and found her worthy of the knowledge. "They lived here while the main house was being built up. I'm just doing some repairs. I'd offer you a drink, but I didn't grab anything but my bag when I rushed down here."

"Tornado, you said."

As if summoned by her stated question, the wind picked up in a howl. The entire home overhead creaked and moaned against the angry weather.

He cocked his head to the side at a noise she didn't catch. At first. Seconds later, boots thudded down the steps and raised dust in the air.

"Lorne?" a second man growled. "You got that idiot on the ATV?"

Sloan bristled at the words. She didn't have the bright idea to go out with dark clouds gathering on the horizon. She had no say in splitting up from her partner.

A slow smile spread across Lorne's face. He didn't even lift his eyes to the newcomer. The scrutiny sparked a bloom of warming tingles at the base of her spine.

"Got her," Lorne answered simply.

LORNE CURSED HIS DUMB LUCK. He'd tried to avoid Bearden, the ranch, and any other living creature after he spotted his cousin in town. Instead, he'd chased off lions trying to scratch up the side of the homestead in some territory dispute, had Alex breathing down his neck, and then heard the telltale sounds of an engine out in the middle of a tornado warning.

Instincts to help anyone caught in the storm kicked into overdrive when he realized it was *her*. His bear roared loudly as soon as her scent reached his nose, and hadn't stopped since.

Alex paused on the bottom step. Lorne's hackles rose the longer Alex stared at the gorgeous woman. Her scent flickered with a hint of worry, though her face didn't show any sign.

Unmarked, unmated, *his*. The other male needed to learn his place.

Lip raised in a snarl, he put himself between the threat and his mate.

Mate. *Mate?* No. Never.

Alex switched his glare from the woman to him. Glowing green eyes replaced those of his human half, but they didn't lose the intelligence that meant an incoming shift. After a second, the other man dropped his gaze a fraction of an inch.

He didn't completely back off or disappear entirely, but Lorne took the win. Alex's bear was a fucking beast, and he didn't need a brawl in such a small space. The human wouldn't stand a chance, and he didn't want more blood on his hands.

"Got the tarp secured over that hole in the roof. Won't last long if this wind keeps up," Alex said, more growl than words. "Who are you?"

Spots of shock and anger colored her cheeks and mingled with her prickling scent. The soft strawberries and cream didn't fade, only thickened into an even more delicious swirl. "Sloan. Kent. And I have people waiting for me back at the office, so don't try anything, Mr...?"

Sloan. Lorne mulled her name over in his mind, savoring it like one of those elitist fools with sips of wine. He didn't want to spit her out and wash her away with another drink. He wanted to drown in the cask.

"Lorne. Bennett," he answered. Alex snapped his mouth shut with a satisfying click. Good. Asshole needed to learn some manners. "Surprised you didn't know that from time spent in your holding cell. This is Alex."

"You're SEA, right?" Alex demanded.

A mark against her, and also a curiosity.

How did she come to work for those bastards? Lorne wanted to know what steps brought her there and if she was as full of loathing for his kind as the hunter jackasses she'd watched brought down the night their paths first crossed.

Her eyes flicked from him to Alex, then back again. Lorne wanted to purr. He couldn't look anywhere else, either.

"A list of names isn't putting them to faces. None of you were booked. Nothing pulled up on the registration list, either."

Damn right. Joss was registered, he thought, but none of the other men had their names on the rolls. Doing so was asking for trouble, and had already bitten more than a few supernaturals in the ass. Crazies looking for a cause were just a few clicks away from a target list. And the Black Claw men? They all had their reasons for keeping their heads low.

"So you looked into me. My, my, that sounds like some abuse of power," Lorne said with a smirk.

Alex looked at him like he'd grown a second head.

Teasing. Him. He'd already said more words to her than his clan in the last week. He wanted to buck the hold she had over him and sink further into it.

Mates were a blessing, weren't they? Ethan and Hunter were better men for finding theirs.

Except he wouldn't enjoy his. Couldn't. Not when he was a dead man whose body just hadn't quit yet.

"Well, you were caught at the location of a suspected shifter trafficker and one of you took an injury. Of course we'd check." She paused, then asked in a softer voice, "The older man, is he okay? I didn't hear anything after he was taken for medical care."

The entire night was one Lorne didn't want to remember. Hunter nearly lost his mind when Joss went missing. The entire clan, plus Hunter's father, closed ranks and searched for her. When it became clear that hunters, fucking scum of the universe, had snatched her up, Lorne felt his heart drop into his stomach. He wouldn't wish losing such a precious treasure on his worst enemy.

His bear rolled through him with strong instincts to hang on tightly to the woman. Lorne shoved down the thoughts as soon as they rose up, but it was like playing whack-a-mole. His idiot inner animal replaced every sending he killed with two more.

Sloan with smiles just for him, her scent heavy in his den, a bite mark on her lovely skin...

Wrapped up in his towel, covering her scent with his own, that felt too right. Too domestic.

And not meant for him.

Lorne cleared his throat as he sank to the floor. "Nothing a good sleep and a shift wouldn't cure." True, too. Once the silver bullet was pulled from Hunter's father's arm, he was good as new.

She nodded once, lips set in a strong line. He respected that she didn't get wishy-washy or went disbelieving. She simply absorbed the information.

Alex still had narrowed eyes when he clomped down the last step and slid to the floor as far from Sloan as the room would allow. "You bring down the radio?"

Lorne's bear wanted to rip the man apart just a little less than before.

He rummaged through his bag until he put fingers on a small radio. He clicked on a local channel. The tail end of emergency warning beeps faded into soft music while the storm continued to rage on above them. "We were listening to this when they broke through with the sighting. We should hear something."

Sloan tugged the towel tighter around herself

and shifted from one foot to the other before she leaned against the slab wall. "At least I know you didn't lure me in here for anything nefarious."

He grunted. He was a lot of things, a killer one of them, but she had nothing to fear from him. Not when his bear was riding him hard to cross the space separating them and claim her thoroughly.

The constant, restless prowling of his inner beast ceased entirely. The roars didn't quiet, nor did the urges to get close to the woman, but it was like a sudden weight lifted from his mind.

*Mate.*

He wanted her. Naked, under him, screaming his name. Her scent clogged up his nose and made the temptation even worse.

He couldn't touch her. Ian was somewhere in town. A human girl was what got him into trouble to begin with. His cousin would see Sloan as another target. If not Ian, then someone else. The Bennett clan had numbers on their side and held grudges better than anyone he knew.

Dead men didn't have mates.

Pain slashed his middle.

"Why were you out riding in the rain, anyway?" he asked through his bear's objections.

"Patrol."

Lorne didn't fake his scowl. Being looked into during a run-in with the law was one thing. Having them peeping over the fence was something entirely different. The whole agency was founded on putting a boot to the throats of those with magic in their veins. New protocols and mission statements didn't erase the damage already done.

"Keeping others out, or us in?" Alex asked with derision stinging his tongue.

Sloan swung her attention to the other man, and Lorne wanted to kill him again.

"Trying to keep everyone safe," she corrected smoothly. "You have two major roads going into town—"

"It's a free country, isn't it? Movement isn't restricted."

Yet. Give them time and opportunity, and Lorne was sure someone would try to contain the supernatural threat.

"No, it's not." Irritation entered her scent. "But someone camping out where they don't belong is at risk. I don't want a trigger-happy camper shooting at a bear in the distance, nor do I want anyone on this side of things to get pissed at a trespasser."

"And we need babysitters with badges to make sure that doesn't happen?" Alex growled.

Oh, she didn't like being called that. Her eyes narrowed and her teeth ground together, and Lorne jumped in before the beastly bear did anything else to upset his mate.

"Alex," Lorne warned.

Sloan flicked a dark look at him as if to say she didn't want or appreciate his help. More irritation flooded her scent when she focused back on Alex.

"We're not the bad guys. I seem to recall we helped your... clan out of a bind just a few days ago."

She stumbled just briefly on the word, like she knew it but wasn't entirely comfortable using it. More SEA training, he supposed.

"Let's not pretend that was out of concern for us. You people were on a mission. We just got caught up in it," Lorne interjected.

"So what if you were? We still put those people in cuffs and hauled them away. Less bad guys on the street is a positive."

And how many had she personally taken off the street? His eyes flicked down to the butt of her gun poking out of the holster on her belt.

She followed his gaze and shrugged. "Go ahead and ask. Everyone wants to, though most are polite enough to keep it to themselves."

Lorne chuckled. Feisty woman, going toe-to-toe

like she couldn't help herself. "Did they teach you to be passive aggressive at the Academy for Ruining Supernatural Lives, or does that just come naturally?"

She grinned with too many teeth. "I prefer straight aggression to the passive shit. *That* comes naturally."

Another small laugh rumbled in his chest. He didn't know why he liked pushing her buttons so much, but there it was. Alex didn't help, but she held her own against him. His bear chuffed with pride at the fierce woman.

And Alex once again looked at him like he was crazy. Fuck him. Maybe he was. But dammit, he wanted to know what made her tick. By the Broken, he wanted to learn the simple things, too, like her favorite flower or movies she loved as a kid or treats when a sweet tooth hit.

"How'd you wind up working for those bastards, anyway?"

Sloan pursed her lips like she wanted to snap something at him. "You're probably going to tell me I'm full of shit, but justice brought me here. I believe it exists for the richest man to the poorest. Human and shifter and every other creature alike."

Lorne grunted. He felt like he'd been kicked in

the chest. Justice. What a joke. There was take and take and take, all of it unfair. Innocents always got hurt. "Pretty words, and not at all how the world works."

She was shaking her head even before he finished. The stubborn set of her jaw that'd tightened when Alex needled her returned. "Then shouldn't we do everything in our power to make it work that way? Sitting by and talking shit is easy. Having the balls to stand up to a bully is the brave change needed."

"Brave isn't always smart. It isn't even always successful." He took a stand for the side of good and right, once. He'd nearly been killed because of it.

The radio crackled again with another interruption. "This just in from our weather team. The tornado warning has been downgraded to a watch. Storms continue to move through the area, but the zones of significant worry have dissipated. Stay safe out there, folks."

"Looks like you're free to go, officer," Alex sniped.

"Agent would be the appropriate term," she shot back.

Lorne rolled to his feet and let off a short sigh. The air was heavy with tension that made his shoulders ache and his skin itch. He wanted to shift, he wanted to reach out and run his hands down Sloan's arms, he wanted Alex gone.

He sure as hell didn't want to let their short time together end. "Let me load your rig up and give you a lift. This rain isn't going to quit anytime soon."

Alex rubbed a hand over his head. "You sure about that with your thing going on?"

Sloan cocked her head, but didn't say a word.

He wanted more time with her. A half hour crouched in a cellar while a storm spun above them wasn't enough. A month wouldn't be enough. He needed a lifetime.

On the other side of his roaring desire was the cold wash of truth. He couldn't drag her into his mess. No matter how tough she seemed. His problems were his own. His fate was already determined. He didn't want to imagine tears welling in those big blue eyes.

He needed to burn the bridge before it was even built. Drive her away, make her want to keep clear of him. If she couldn't stand the sight of him, his bear would need to accept they weren't meant to be.

There was no future with the woman. No seeing what they each liked.

Claws sank into his chest as his beast tore him apart from the inside out.

Lorne swallowed hard and kicked his bear to the back of his head. Instincts be damned. He could ask his questions and give her a ride, but that was where the line was drawn.

Weak man. Weak bear. He had to be strong to keep her safe. Safe meant away from him.

But he couldn't get her words out of his head. Justice. The Bennetts thought they were serving it, but it was a plate spoiled by years of mistreatment and war. He could understand it, to an extent. Kick a dog enough and eventually, he'll bite back.

"Yeah," he told Alex gruffly. "And after, we can finish up here and head back to the ranch."

He'd stood by with a shit attitude for long enough. Ian and the rest of his family could come for him. They could still put him down. But he wasn't going to sit around and wait for it to happen.

Maybe it was time to bite.

# CHAPTER 5

S loan drummed her fingers against the table in front of her and waited for Crewe to enter the briefing room. Her shift was just about over, but with such a small unit, Crewe liked to brief everyone during the overlap. Said he couldn't stand repeating himself.

August leaned closer and bumped her with his shoulder. "You got plans for the festival?"

Summertime Fest, as the folks in Bearden called it. The entire thing was a raucous mess, from what she'd been told. Fair food and rides during the day, music and other activities at night. Fireworks were even scheduled for the Fourth of July.

"Nothing formal. You?"

"Probably take the mate and cubs on my day off.

The boys are dying to get on that damn roller coaster that dangles you upside down. They were too short last year. Might just pay off the workers to boost the sign up a few inches so their mom doesn't get worried. She'd prefer if they stay on the spinning teacups for the rest of their lives."

Sloan huffed a laugh. "My mom was the opposite. She couldn't wait for me to do the thrill rides. Dad was the one who tossed everything if he spun around too fast."

Something had shifted with her status since the storm. Lorne hadn't bumped across the land for very long before her radio crackled with a hint of panic in August's voice. Apparently, no one in the office wanted to be responsible for their only human agent being blown away during a rare tornado.

That she hadn't caved during the storm or complained about fending for herself proved she wasn't weak. They were almost treating her like an equal. August had thawed the most, but the suspicious looks from the rest had just about disappeared.

Crewe blew past in his usual clipped pace. "Quiet down, quiet down. We have a lot to discuss before everyone heads out." Crewe rustled his papers and tapped them into order against the podium. "Rumors from our counterparts across the enclave line say a delegation from a nearby fae court will be attending the Summertime Fest. The Bearden PD has graciously asked us to help with security. No one wants a repeat of what happened last time."

Heads nodded all around the room as Sloan raised her eyebrows. "What happened last time?"

August snorted. "Oh, just a little fae fuckery and outing our entire existence to you humans."

Sloan frowned. Back to square one.

"Don't forget the dragon fire," someone else muttered.

Working for the feds was a different beast than working as a beat cop. Still, she found it hard to police a population when she knew so little about them. Their holidays, their stories, even their public history were more nuanced than she gleaned from reading reports and articles. She'd moved into the enclave to jumpstart her knowledge, but she still felt like an outsider ninety percent of the time.

She needed someone on call to pick their brain. She needed an informant. Instead of snitching on fellow criminals, she wanted to dig in and learn about the people of Bearden.

Sloan drummed her fingers once again. Maybe she had an in with someone. Someone she owed a huge thank you.

Lorne had run circles through her mind in the days since he manhandled her into the cellar. He was hot, yeah. All six-plus, muscled feet of him. And broody in a way that didn't make her roll her eyes. His stretches of quiet were interesting. He wasn't checked out in the slightest; he saw everything that went on around him.

He'd barely spoken after they left the cellar, but she'd felt watched during the entire drive. Not in a creepy sort of way, either. More like he worked to puzzle her out, the same as she tried with him. His raw intensity filled up the cab of his truck.

Talking to him about the town might be excuse enough to get close to him and figure out what went on in his head.

"Snow, you and Kent are to coordinate with Bearden PD. I want a plan on my desk tomorrow." Crewe checked off an item on his list and nodded.

Sloan shot a wide-eyed look to August. Holy shit, an actual assignment. She wanted to run outside and see if the sky was still blue and water hadn't become air.

August held out his fist and she bumped it. Something good came out of that twister.

Crewe continued, "In other news, some young buck looking to make a name for himself this election cycle is floating the idea of forced registration. We've also received requests for the numbers on recidivists. Might mean a push to cut back the three-strike rule."

The attitude of the room immediately chilled. Sloan didn't blame them. Forced registration had been tossed around from the start of the registration list. The three-strike rule was the compromise. Supernaturals were given three warnings before the SEA stepped in to solve the problem if the local authorities refused to act. Stripping away even that much power would step on the toes of police forces and clan hierarchy alike.

The Agency was already seen as overreaching to most folks. They'd earned the reputation, too, no thanks to assholes like her former partner and his suspect-beating ways. The olive branch of a shifter squad would be cut and burned to ash if the rules changed.

Fucking bosses. They always seemed to pull the exact move that made everyone's job harder.

"Now, I'm sure I don't need to remind ~~to remind~~ anyone, but I will say it in case your brains dripped out of your ears overnight. As always, the position of the Agency is that we will uphold the laws of the land." Crewe narrowed his eyes on each of them in turn until the groans quieted. "I don't want a single damn word saying otherwise getting out to the media folks. Do me a favor and watch your damn mouths. Dismissed."

OFF DUTY and full of greasy, delicious diner fare, Sloan checked both ways before jogging across the street. She had it on good authority from the diner's owner that dessert from the coffee shop was the best way to fill the last remaining space in her stomach. Tommy also said to make sure she said that, so Faith would know he wasn't stealing her customers.

The woman in question turned on a bright smile as soon as Sloan walked through the door. "Welcome to Mug Shot. Be right with you."

Sloan stifled a laugh as she took in the decorations. A group of teenagers giggled as they snapped photos of each other in oversized prison-stripe shirts and wrote rude messages in chalk on a board meant to identify a suspect. Other photos were pinned to a corkboard and advertised the "Most Wanted" faces of Bearden.

Behind the counter wasn't immune from the decor, either. The menu board was black with white lettering, and the aprons of the two women working were striped, too. Of all the theme establishments she'd heard of, Mug Shot was definitely her favorite. Bias be damned.

A dark hat bounced by the window and she jerked to attention. Like a puppet on a string, she turned to keep the man in sight.

Yep, she'd recognize that sauntering gait and his wide shoulders anywhere. They'd only crossed through her dreams for several nights straight.

Sloan quickly worked through her half-formed plans to casually cross paths with Lorne and give him her thanks. None jumped out to her as the way to ease into asking him to give her a leg up around town.

"What can I get for you?" A barista murmured behind her. Her nametag read Kate when Sloan turned back to the counter.

"Hey, so this might sound weird, but do you know what he likes?" She jerked her thumb over her shoulder and toward Lorne.

Mom always said the way to a man's heart was through his stomach. Her father always rubbed a hand over his belly and kissed her cheek in indulgent agreement.

A pang of sadness socked Sloan right in her

heart. They were a good couple, her folks. Supported one another through thick and thin. She missed her father like crazy and wanted to live up to his memory.

Even more, she wanted to find her place in the world. The tension in her new unit was beginning to fade. Maybe she could make a life for herself in Bearden.

Justice for all, and a happy home at the end of the day.

The idea was daunting. She'd tried everywhere else she'd been assigned, and failed. She was tired of being the outsider.

Kate followed the direction she jerked her thumb, then a knowing smile spread across her face. "Lorne? Yeah. Massive sweet tooth on that man. The chocolate blackouts are his favorite."

Sloan felt her blood sugar cringe when she checked out the label on the chocolate cookies with chocolate chunks and garnished with chocolate syrup. "Perfect. I'll take a half dozen of those."

Her heart pounded against her breastbone as soon as she hit the sidewalk. Stupid. Silly. He hadn't even looked at her, and she quaked worse than when Barry Sutton asked her to the school dance in sixth grade.

Sure, the man was pure sex. She'd be insane to not be attracted to him. Snug jeans clung to his powerful legs so tight she doubted she could even slip her hand into a back pocket. Those big muscles and scruffed up cheeks belonged in an underwear ad.

The state of her empty bed wasn't the concern at that moment. She owed him a thank you. Even if he didn't want to speak with her any further than that, he'd helped her out of a bind and moved her off desk duty.

"Lorne! Hey, wait up!"

He whirled around, wide eyes holding just a tinge of shock that disappeared quickly. His entire frame seemed to relax when he tipped the brim of his hat. "Agent Kent," he rumbled. "Nice to see you dried out."

Fire blazed under her skin as he dipped his gaze down her body. A thrum picked up the beat of her heart, right between her legs. Professional, she reminded herself, but that needy part of her wasn't convinced.

Sloan cleared her throat. "I, uh, wanted to thank you for the other day."

A simmering smile spread across his face. "Nothing to it."

"Well, it was something to me. I asked at the coffee shop, and the barista said you liked these. So, thank you." She shoved the black-and-white striped box at him.

Eyebrows shooting together, he lifted the top of the box and peeked inside. "You didn't have to do this."

"I wanted to."

"You always do everything you want?"

"When I'm not following orders."

Holy hell. The words tumbled out of her mouth before she had a chance to consider them. Well, shit. No taking them back now that they were alive.

Lorne's lips quirked into a hot as sin smirk that had her suddenly blushing. Blushing! Like she was some sweet little girl from next door, and not a snitch bitch struggling to figure out where she stood with her new assignment.

He stiffened suddenly. His nostrils flared and his eyes brightened to a glowing gold. He stared at something over her shoulder hard enough for her to turn and see what was running for them.

"What?" she asked when she twisted back around.

"Nothing," he growled. "Just thought I saw someone in the crowd."

Before she could ask, he shook himself and tilted his head to the side. His hand reached out and touched the small of her back. "Come on. Let's get off the sidewalk. You been down to the river?"

Sloan trailed after him even when the light pressure and wave of heat against her back lifted. "Just what I've seen from the back patio of the barbecue place."

"Are you staying in town? I thought most of your kind were living near the office."

"Some are here, others are in the surrounding towns. I wanted to get a feel for the people I'm supposed to watch over."

"Yeah? And what have you observed, Agent?" He opened the box as they walked and offered her the first choice.

"Sloan, please. I'm not on duty." She tucked a flyaway strand of hair behind her ear and regretted not putting her hair up before she left her house. Well, she hadn't expected to meet with the man. She probably looked like a hot mess in her tank top and skinny jeans with holes at the knees. She didn't know how to be girly or stylish. Throwing her hair into a bun for work was the height of her skill.

She took a cookie and chewed slowly to give herself time to think. Offending him with something off the cuff wouldn't help her any. "It's a slower pace than I'm used to. I come from a big city. Never worked a place with under a hundred thousand people in the limits."

"Don't worry. We get into our fair share of trouble."

"Like bundling women into your basement?"

A deep chuckle spilled from his lips, but didn't quite reach his eyes. Those, he cast over her head and back toward the main road.

Didn't want to be seen with a human, maybe? Or was it because of where she worked? Neither option bode well for mining his knowledge.

Lorne led her off the town square and down a path next to Town Hall. A few others strolled along the path with them. Witnesses combined with the fact that he'd already had a chance for misdeeds eased her woman-alone doubts. Besides, she trusted him. The same gut instinct that said he wasn't a danger to her reared its head again.

Trees shaded most of the well-worn walk. Flowering bushes lined the path, manicured just enough to maintain an appearance of wild beauty without becoming an overgrown mess. It wasn't long before she heard the bubbling of rushing water.

Benches sat near the riverbank, and she made her

way to one. Lorne lowered himself next to her and stretched his arm over the back of the bench. Sloan resisted the urge to scoot closer or lean into the hand inches from her shoulder. So close, she couldn't possibly miss his scent. Manly, like worked leather and cologne, he smelled divine.

Professional, she reminded herself. She needed an ear on the inside, someone to answer any stupid questions.

She'd talked to countless witnesses and suspects in her line of work, but none had her tongue-tied as much as the cowboy at her side. "Saved anyone else stranded by storms?"

"Only you." His lips picked up on one side. "No one else that idiotic has come along since."

The words held no sting and the twinkling in his eyes made the tease clear. Her pulse leaped.

"Careful. I've tossed men into lockup for less."

He snorted, but the smile continued to spread across his face and she had the distinct feeling that he approved of her answer.

He dug out another cookie and finished it in two bites. "What did you track me down for?"

"As embarrassing as it is to admit, I've had some trouble getting a foothold around here. I don't know my way around. I was hoping you could help me get my bearings."

He laughed. "You want me to be your C.I."

"That's not—"

"It is." He tapped his nose. "Don't lie to me, sweetheart. You want an informant. Why?"

"Like I said. I don't know my way around here. I don't know the terrain, I don't know the people, and I don't know how to get people to see beyond the uniform. I don't want to be just a badge. I want to be someone that's trusted."

He cocked his head to the side and looked at her so intently she thought he could read her mind. Maybe he could. More likely, she was just that transparent. He cut through all her pleasant chit-chat and working up to the big ask.

"Knowing the facts of a place aren't going to get you any closer to being part of them. You'll never be part of them. You're human."

Human. Outsider. Not where she belonged.

"I guess that's it, then." She pushed to her feet and nodded to him as she passed. Disappointment crackled within her, and not just at her outsider status. He called it out, probably felt it himself. She wouldn't let him see how the words stung. "Thanks for everything."

Lorne's hand wrapped around her wrist and spun her back around. Eyes blazing and a devilish smile lifting his lips, Lorne stepped into her space. She didn't have a chance for shock or questions before he lowered his face and kissed her.

Sloan's brain shorted out. Her skin buzzed with electricity wherever they touched. He started slow, skimming his mouth across hers in a gentle, sipping taste. Then a groan rumbled in his chest, vibrated through her, and she was lost.

Oh, lordy. Her toes curled in her sneakers as his fingers dug into her hair. His other hand planted against the small of her back and tugged her closer. His beard scratched at her soft skin when he nipped at her lower lip.

Stop. She needed to stop.

Sloan parted her lips the moment his tongue brushed against them. Slow sips were quickly discarded with tangled tongues and deep licks. Heat roared through her veins and she groaned with the ache he ignited in her. It went deeper than just wanting to get him back to her home, or on the bench, or against a tree. She wanted to peel back all his layers and see what lay underneath.

Daring, to grab an agent and take her into a dark basement while griping the entire time. Cautious, with his secretive looks over his shoulder. Intuitive man with a sweet tooth.

Lorne groaned again, more growl than natural noise, and Sloan added another interesting observation to the pile.

Shifter.

Growly, sexy, shifter who probably wouldn't be intimidated by her in the slightest.

Lorne's fingers tightened on her for a split second before he eased away. His lips grazed the shell of her ear. "I won't be your informant, but I will help you around. Make this place your home, then you'll be one of them."

One of 'them.' Never 'one of us.' Sloan stashed away that little nugget to pick at later.

Lorne dipped the brim of his cowboy hat. Gold eyes sparkled at her from the shadows. "Until next time... Sloan."

Heat pooled in her middle with his deep, sexy chuckle.

# CHAPTER 6

She'd kissed him. Holy crap, she'd kissed a shifter.

Hot cowboy shifter, no less.

Still a shifter. Still one that might need watching.

What had the other one—Alex—asked? Was she in charge of keeping them in, or others out?

Right then, she wasn't in charge of a damn thing. And she was acting like a complete fool. Over a single kiss.

Sloan stared at her reflection in the mirror of her Jeep and passed a finger over her lips. Idiot. She couldn't still feel Lorne's lips on her own. She glared at herself and hopped down to the ground. Duty called, and daydreams needed to be banished. She wouldn't be one of those girls that let a man distract her when he wasn't even around.

She trailed between desks starting to populate with those on duty on her way to the break room for morning coffee. Eyes followed her, sending her heart into a quicker pace. She felt like the teen girl in all those coming-of-age movies.

Sloan rolled her eyes and added creamer to her drink. No, no one could tell she'd popped her shifter-kissing cherry. *She* was making things weird by casting furtive looks all around.

She thought of pulling Crewe aside and spilling her guts to him. Flirting wasn't expressly forbidden. Dating, either. Agents had lives outside of work.

But getting involved with someone she wanted to pump for information? Someone in the community she was tasked with overseeing? Those were some murky areas.

Except, she wouldn't be using Lorne for information. He made it clear he wouldn't be an informant of any kind. A friend who showed her around town, helped her find her footing, yes. Someone she could use, no. His words and his kiss both cleared and created an ethical dilemma she didn't want to face.

Then there was the possibility of losing face with

the rest of the unit. They might see her admission as a sign of shame.

Any move she made seemed designed to knock her feet out from under her. She'd learned to tread lightly. Girl cops had to watch themselves for fear of being seen as weak or incapable. Sole human working with a bunch of super-strength shifters was the same role she'd played her entire career.

"Morning," she greeted August as she took her seat. He grunted in response and dug into the breakfast burrito in his hands.

No conversation happening while he devoured his meal with sounds of affection she doubted she'd ever heard a man make for her, Sloan reached for the few items delivered to her desk before she arrived. They were surprisingly and pleasantly low in number—a message confirming a meeting late in the afternoon with the Bearden Chief of Police, a request for information on a case from her former unit, and a sealed envelope at the bottom of the pile.

Sloan turned the last over and over, tonguing her teeth as she studied it. A stamp, but no processing through the post office. No return address, either. She didn't recognize the handwriting, but she hadn't recognized the last letter full of dried up snake skins, either.

Her fingers caught under the edges before she had another second to think. Dread and anger filled her belly as she ripped the paper apart.

A photo fluttered to the floor.

Sloan stooped to pick it up. Shock scalded her skin the moment she turned it over.

Her and Lorne, faces pressed together, utterly unaware of anyone snapping the picture.

*Motherfucker.*

Sloan glanced up to see if anyone had spotted her, then stuffed the picture back into the envelope, and the envelope into her pocket.

Jimmy and his band of fuckheads were at it again, making sure she knew she was watched.

August arched an eyebrow at her. "You good?"

"Never better."

This shit was her problem. She wouldn't give them the satisfaction of asking for protection. They wanted her scared, and she refused to even blink.

The picture was proof she still had a target on her back. Someone had to follow her and get close enough to snap such a thing. And what the fuck was the message behind it? They could get to her anywhere? She should be ashamed of getting close to someone?

Or was it a direct threat against the man himself?

Sloan didn't know which way to turn. None of her options felt right.

Did she run into the arms of a man she barely knew, and who might head for the hills the moment she didn't swoon when he wanted? More than one man couldn't keep up with her lifestyle and she refused to be some simpering, needy woman. Not many would stick around knowing she brought threats into their lives.

Did she lean on her new coworkers, some who still shot suspicious looks when they thought she wasn't looking? She wasn't one of them. She didn't have an animal under her skin. Hell, even her placement in the unit was still a raw subject to some.

Looking to her old unit was just as disastrous. Most were happy to see the Snitch Bitch gone. Someone there kept tabs for Jimmy Culpepper and his band of assholes. Until she knew who to trust, she couldn't make asks of anyone.

Best she leave Lorne out of things, too. Hot as that kiss was and as much as she looked forward to getting to know the, ah, *town*, she wasn't safe for him. Forgetting his slow smiles and solid chest were better than dragging him into her issues.

Like anything else in her life, she'd tough it out.

They'd get bored when they realized she wouldn't give them any reaction.

Creaking chairs shook her out of her thoughts. Right. Morning briefing.

Sloan followed August into the room with the rest of the unit. Crewe already stood at the ready, looking more carved of stone than usual.

"All right, down to business. Last night, we received word of an assault on a human family in a campground about sixty miles east of here. Father was badly injured, possibly bitten." Crewe spat out the last words. "Mother and daughter received minor wounds."

Everyone in the room shifted in their seats. More than one face glared straight ahead with jaws clenched.

To them, the assault wasn't the worst of the problem. The bite meant a forced change, and that meant certain death for the culprit and risk of it for the victim. The shifter population didn't put up with rogue individuals chomping down and creating more indiscriminately.

Rumors of drugs to reverse bitten shifters existed, but those were whispered about with hope and praise by hunters more than anyone with a lick of sense. Sloan didn't want to add madmen with needles to her list of worries. Shifters free with their teeth were enough.

A picture flashed up behind Crewe. "We're looking for this man. Ian Bennett. He hails from a bear clan in Oklahoma, but was recently spotted in our neck of the woods. As far as we can tell, his clan fell apart between five to ten years ago. Their alpha disappeared, probably in some challenge fight, and the families inside have peeled off and moved on. Only a handful remain in the original territory. Ian here has a love of drinking, driving, fist fights, and skipping out on court dates."

Sloan nearly sputtered. "Bennett. Like Lorne Bennett? From our friends at Black Claw?"

"One and the same, though from what they told us when we had them here, he hasn't been home in twelve years. Could be Ian is looking up his relative. Could be he's just wanted to relocate to the enclave."

August looked at her with suspicion, then snapped his attention back to Crewe. "Kent and I can head out and ask him some questions."

Crewe nodded. "Good. The rest of you, keep your eyes peeled. We don't need this fucker putting a damper on the upcoming festival."

# CHAPTER 7

Lorne could barely focus on the humans dismounting in the paddock. They were full of laughter and jokes after a successful trail ride. The next stop of their day would be a small feast prepared by the ranch chef, Joss.

The noise of the guests contrasted with the thoughts rumbling in his head, though. Sticking around happy couples didn't appeal to him in the slightest. They were just another reminder of what he couldn't have.

Sloan's face pushed out all other thoughts. His insides clenched with the need to be near her and the instinct to protect. Anyone else, and those two would mean the same thing. He wasn't anyone else.

Lorne nodded kindly to the man closest to him

and reached for the reins to lead his mount into the barn with his own. The animals needed care. That didn't stop because his head and heart wanted different things. The barn was a safer haven than the paddock full of people.

On the other side of the barn, in a smaller pen, he spotted Alex. Surprising. He usually made himself scarce during tour arrivals and departures. The young calf he was feeding slurped the last of her bottle, then bounded away in a show of play. One or two needed extra attention every season, and Alex always volunteered for the job.

A husband and wife pair strayed closer to the fence as Lorne guided both horses into their stalls. With the top doors thrown open, he heard Alex growl, "Back off. She's not for petting."

"Alex," Ethan warned from across the yard.

"No problem. We didn't know," the man stated.

Lorne scrubbed a hand through his hair and settled his Stetson back on his head.

Fuck, what made him kiss Sloan? And before that, lead her anywhere they could be close? Oh, he knew. The messy hair and swell of her breasts above the neck of her tank top. Her delicious scent. Just the memory had blood rushing straight to his cock.

Pure lust had him drooling over her and ignoring

all the signs that slapped him in the face. He'd gone into town to look for Ian and found Sloan instead. The whiff of his cousin's scent should have been enough to put distance between him and anyone he cared about. The human woman, especially, needed protection from his family. They'd done a number on Lilah. He couldn't let them do the same to Sloan.

His bear prowled through his mind, swiping at unseen dangers. Lorne wanted to put an end to the entire mess. He'd been waiting too long, living his life looking over his shoulder. There was no moving forward with the demons of the past dragging him backward.

The eased tension that Sloan gave him drowned under the roaring of his inner beast. He couldn't talk the bear down. Work and clan were unwanted distractions. He needed to hunt down any possible threats to Sloan.

At his low growl, Nova tossed her head. Lorne stroked a hand down the mare's neck to calm the agitation she'd picked up from him. He went through the motions of brushing her down and gave her an extra scratch on the rump for putting up with him before moving to another horse needing care.

"The fuck was that about?" Jesse asked in the next stall.

Alex paced in the small box of a third stall. Growls sawed out of him with each huffed breath. "It's those fucking tourists. They come in here, acting like they own the place. Why the fuck can't we keep them from wandering?"

"Easy," Jesse muttered. "They backed off, that's what counts."

There was a loud thump. Alex kicking the door of the stall, probably. "We're the ones that live here. I'm sick of them messing with everything."

Someone needed to step in before Alex blew his lid. Too many unfamiliar eyes were around to stand witness.

His bear bunched under his skin. Lorne slid a glance to Ethan, then to Hunter. They remained oblivious to the trouble brewing right next to them. Hunter helped settle the mounts while Ethan yammered with the guests.

Lorne shook his head and went back to work. Someone had to make nice with the tourists and usher them to their next activities.

Maybe he should have stayed at the homestead. Tussling with lions determined to get a rise out of Ethan was better than mooning over a woman he couldn't have.

His bear roared loud enough to bring pained tears to his eyes.

Giving Sloan a lift was one thing. Accepting her gifted cookies and then kissing her flirted with disaster. He was a dead man walking. Ian hunted him. Toyed with him, more like. Getting near Sloan put a target on her back.

He was certain she'd kick him in the shins if he even suggested she needed to be kept safe.

His lips twitched with a smile before he chained down the good feeling. Lorne chanted a reminder to his inner beast before the bear could snap at his control.

*No tears. Don't leave anyone behind.*

Besides, she was on the wrong side of the law for a man like him. He had blood on his hands. All her pretty words about making the world a just place wouldn't wash him clean.

He scowled at the hay underfoot and rolled his shoulders. His skin felt too tight. His bear wanted out, despite his reasoning. Couldn't do that. The beast would run straight for Sloan.

*Bite. Mark. Claim.*

Not happening. Not when Ian could hurt her to wound him.

Lorne wanted to taste her again. He wanted her

delicious scent filling his nose and her soft groans in his ear. Ian and all the other Bennetts stood in the way of those wishes. Lorne had to figure his shit out before getting near Sloan again. He didn't want more blood on his hands.

Another thump of a fist hitting wood grabbed his attention. Lorne lifted his eyes to find Alex pacing in the middle of the breezeway and throwing dark looks toward the trail riders still milling outside the barn doors.

The man's fists clenched. "I'm just saying, maybe he needs to focus more on his own damn people than every asshole who wants to play cowboy for the day."

"Get your head out of your ass, or get the fuck out of the barn," Jesse hissed.

"Don't pull that alpha crap with me," Alex snarled in answer. "You're not in charge."

"You're not either. Besides," Hunter snarked as he passed with a saddle meant for the tack room. "He lets you play cowboy every day."

Alex roared, and his monster of a bear ripped out of his skin. Hunter didn't have enough time to shift before Alex was on him, snapping huge jaws on the arm he threw over his face to protect himself. By the time he'd changed shape, there was nothing but fury in his eyes.

"Motherfucker," Jesse swore.

Lorne silently echoed the curse. He should have paid more attention. Done more. Triggered a brawl in the morning before all the humans showed up to see their wild sides.

Wasn't that proof enough that Sloan was bad news? She clogged up his head and left him distracted. The delicate balance he kept over himself and the others was in shambles.

Alex and Hunter backed up slowly, huge paws striking out at one another as they stepped through the barn. Jesse passed a hand over his face and shot a look to the humans murmuring and pointing from the very edges of the building.

"Back up!" Lorne shouted. He threw his arms wide and herded the group away from the barn doors. "Give them room!"

Ethan sprinted toward them, murder written across his expression. Tansey and Joss were hot on his heels and tried to corral the humans to no avail. Cell phones were out and pointed right at the brawling bears.

"Shift back!" Ethan yelled. "I swear to all that's holy, I will skin you both alive!"

Power whipped off Ethan with enough furious

force that both Lorne and Jesse doubled over. The mates, too, paled and looked sick. Hunter's shift ripped through him faster than it started and left the man panting in the dirt, red streaked across his skin.

Alex, beast that he was, shook his head like he'd simply been stung by a bee. He scratched long claws into the earth and lifted his lips in a snarl.

Shit.

Too many eyes watching. Too many records being made. Alex was unstable enough to throw down for alpha of the clan, and Ethan was powerful enough to put him down permanently. Neither were scenes that needed to play across any screen with an internet connection.

"I said *shift*," Ethan growled in a low voice.

The words were thick with alpha order. Lorne stumbled before he locked his knees against the onslaught.

Alex shook his head again, then, blessedly melted back from bear to man.

Ethan didn't give him a second to recover. He knelt by Alex and growled another order into his ear. "Get the fuck back to your hut. Do not leave until I say."

With a final snarl, Alex pushed haltingly to his feet. His shoulders stayed straight and tight as he lurched away from the barn, naked as the day he was born.

The air left Lorne's lungs as soon as Alex disappeared from sight. The others, too, let go of unsteady breaths. They seemed loud over the murmurings of the gathered crowd.

"That's a wrap! Hope everyone enjoyed a preview of our newest attraction! Tell all your friends about BWE. That's Bear Wrestling Entertainment." Tansey stomped toward the house, then turned back when no one followed. "Well? Who wants some food?"

"Dangerous," someone murmured as the group started to shuffle toward the house.

"Maybe they should be kept to their towns," another guest voiced.

Ian wasn't the only danger to a human like Sloan. One wrong move and Alex could kill someone. Bringing a federal agent onto the ranch wasn't in anyone's best interests. Alex would be thrown on the damn registration list by the end of the first day and earn himself a one-way ticket to Shiftermax by the end of the week. No way would he survive that potential death camp.

Sloan was too good for his life. His was messy, destructive, wild. There was no room for sweet justice when they were just barely hanging on to sanity.

THE SECOND THE SUV bumped around the last bend of Black Claw's long driveway, Sloan spotted him. Lorne lifted his head from the back of a pickup, slowly straightening and eyeing the SUV with a blank expression. The long seconds merged into a full moment before he waved a hand in acknowledgment and turned back to his task.

Sloan couldn't force herself to look away. His arms and back flexed as he picked up a load of wood posts like they weighed nothing and carried them into the barn.

Sloan cocked her head to the side and watched with utter appreciation the way his jeans molded to his backside. Damn. No one could compete with that show of strength and casual confidence.

August jabbed an elbow into her side. "Keep it in your pants, Kent."

"Fuck off," she snapped back.

Well, that cleared one thing up. August wasn't shooting any disapproval her way.

Lorne reappeared from the darkened barn opening, slapping his hands against his jeans and raising a cloud of dust that did little to wipe away the stains of hard labor.

A smile spread across his face as she stepped out of the SUV and, hand to heart, Sloan thought hers skipped a beat. She wanted to traipse through a field of fucking flowers with the man. Thoughts of being swept off her feet and then loved more than August loved his morning breakfast burrito were in full force.

"You here about the fight?"

"Fight? What fight?" Sloan looked around. Now that he mentioned it, the load of fence posts made sense. Wood in a few spots looked newer than the others. "Something we should know?"

"Never mind." Lorne took off his hat and ran his fingers through his hair. His shoulders relaxed a fraction and he flashed her a smile. "Didn't think you'd be around so soon," he said with a voice velvety enough to melt her core.

"What can I say? I'm not one for waiting."

Next to her, August made a sound much too close to a snort for her comfort.

Professional. She was a professional on professional duty. Being hit so hard with lust that she trembled wasn't the image she wanted to present.

She pressed her lips together and tried her best to ignore the fine hairs lifting all over her body. "Got a couple questions for you. Do you know an Ian Bennett?"

Lorne's sexy smile faltered, then disappeared into a scowl. "What of it?"

The switch he pulled scratched at her instincts. She'd watched suspects go from bright and happy to raging at the drop of a hat. Lorne didn't look like he'd be throwing a chair at the two-way glass—yet—but he certainly wasn't pleased with the line of questioning.

"Don't know if you heard, but a family was assaulted in a campground a ways from here. Your man Ian might know something about it."

"Not my man, not my friend, not my anything. And you should stay out of it." Lorne's tone turned cold. His eyes, so warm and welcoming moments earlier, hardened into shards of black ice.

Stay out of it? Like hell she would. The order and sudden change of personality made her want to dig.

She slouched and slipped her thumbs through her belt loops. Just a casual cop asking some casual questions. "Have you had any contact with Ian in the last few weeks?"

"Haven't talked to him in years, and I wouldn't

want to. I left that entire clan of dickweavils behind when I moved this way."

August slid her a look, then focused back on Lorne. "That was when, exactly?"

"Seven or eight years in the enclave," Lorne answered tightly.

"And before that?"

He shrugged up one shoulder. "Oh, here and there."

Sloan opened her mouth to push harder when she caught sight of another man rounding the barn. Ethan or Jesse, he had to be. She could put names to faces of three of the clan, but the other two were still a mystery.

He strode up to Lorne, face stony, and crossed his arms over his chest. "There a problem?"

"No problem, alpha," Lorne said quickly. "They were just leaving."

"Just asking a few questions," Sloan said over him.

Alpha. That had to be Ethan, then.

She lifted her chin and addressed the Black Claw leader. "We're trying to locate Ian Bennett."

"Only Bennett I know is Lorne."

"Have you talked with anyone else that might

know where we could find Ian? Anyone from your birth clan?" August asked.

Lorne's jaw set in a hard line and his eyes churned with gold. "Keep out of it. If Ian shows up, he's my problem. Not yours."

"Why would he be a problem?" Sloan probed.

Lorne muttered something under his breath and hidden in a growl.

August waited a beat, then dropped the big news. "Someone got turned in the attack. That makes him *our* problem."

"If that's the case, then he's even more my problem than before."

His words sent a chill up her spine. "Not true."

"And what are you going to do, officer? Get yourself bit or killed?"

Jerk.

The words stung, both because they were true and came from him. After their little talks and riverside rendezvous, he didn't see her as anything but a weak human who didn't belong.

Frustration boiled over and left her with a growl. "Agent," she snapped in correction.

Ethan stepped between them. Silver eyes glared first at August, then found her. "Unless you have some papers stating otherwise, I think it's best you leave."

August raised his hands in silent agreement and took a single step back. Sloan stared at Lorne for another long look, not wanting to back down so easily. Weak human who couldn't hold a candle to the strength of her shifter colleagues had to have a spine of steel.

What she found on his face surprised her. Irritated, keeping a wall around himself, yes. But something nearing respect shined in the gold eyes he kept focused on her when she finally stalked toward the SUV.

Sloan chewed on her lower lip while studying the retreating backs of the Black Claw men. "He's hiding something. I think the other one knows what it is, too."

August arched his brows, but kept watch with her. "How do you know that? You can't smell a lie."

"It's almost like I've done this job before." She glared at her partner. "You know, we were doing police work long before we knew walking lie detectors existed."

"If you can call it work," August flashed a grin, then sobered. "Could just be bad blood. What to do about him?"

She turned the puzzles pieces over in her mind and tried to fit them together. She had more missing holes than actual pieces and no clear picture. "I don't think he's going to help our guy, but he's not going to cough up information on him, either. Let's keep a watch and see if there's any contact made."

# CHAPTER 8

"I want my horses back by the end of the day!"

Lorne resisted the urge to rub his temples. Or press a hand to his stomach. Or let his bear rip out of his skin and take to the woods after covering his snout in blood.

Days since Sloan made her dramatic entrance into and exit from his life, and he hated everything. The sun glared at him viciously, the land wavered in his vision, even the scent of the fields and cows and fucking lions in front of him soured his stomach.

"That's not the agreement, Trent," he reasoned.

"Fuck the agreement. I'm not having my horses injured because you fuckers can't keep claws under wraps," Trent growled.

"None of the horses were ever in danger of that. Believe me, we wouldn't hurt them."

Sloan wasn't his problem, though. Not at that moment. No, right then he needed to focus on placating the alpha of the neighboring lion pride. Trent and Ethan were at each other's throats a good portion of the time, but neither could deny they needed each other. Trent had the horses and Ethan had the patience to deal with humans. The trail riding business Black Claw ran wouldn't exist without cooperation. Without that cash flow, the ranch wouldn't last a year.

The situation wasn't as dire now that Tansey had bullied the clan into behaving themselves enough for tourists to stay the night, but the trail rides were still a major draw. Sleepovers in the big house paired better with playing cowboy on horseback than nothing at all. Even the side attraction of mud and trucks wouldn't make up for the loss of horses and dirt.

"No, you're just willing to throw down in front of humans." Trent leaned over and spat after the word.

Behind him, two of his lions shifted in their saddles. Their eyes bounced over him and the land, never once resting. Crazy bastards, just like their alpha.

"We got our problems, same as you," he said calmly.

No use denying what happened. The news buzzed through Bearden and out into the great wide world within hours. Tansey shouted at them over the first guest cancellation, then subsided when reservations picked up in greater numbers. Lorne wasn't sure he liked being the subject of curiosity and hope for a brawl. Then again, that brought the tourists to town in the first place.

"Same as you, we need money to put food on our plates. Taking the horses now will hurt all our people."

Trent glared, but stayed silent while he mulled over his options. Finally, he scratched at the day's growth of stubble along his jaw. "I want ten percent more. Hazard for my mounts."

Lorne shook his head. "You know that's unreasonable."

"Five, then."

"Two."

"Three."

"Three it is," Lorne agreed.

He'd add it all from his own paycheck. He owed Ethan this small favor. Oil and water, that was his alpha and Trent. Lorne could soothe bruised egos and keep the fragile partnership from snapping entirely.

Lorne stuck his hand out to seal the deal.

One by one, heads cocked at the low rumble in the distance. Lorne's heart sank to his stomach. *Not now,* he begged the universe. *Please, not now.*

An ATV poked over a hill in the distance. Instead of turning and running along the patrol route the SEA had set up, the little madwoman on the back zipped straight toward them.

"The fuck is this?" Trent hissed.

Lorne heeled his horse forward, cutting off Trent from Sloan. "Nothing about you."

"Damn right. I wouldn't have any dealings with those traitors and murderers. Why the fuck are they near my land?"

"Near isn't on," Lorne muttered.

Crazy lion. He had his reasons, but damn. Keeping on with so much hate in his heart wasn't doing him or his pride any good. Living next to a bunch of shifters ready to blow up made Lorne's bear remember days with the Bennett clan. His inner beast wanted to get in on the ripping, roaring, clawing insanity.

Lorne ground his teeth together and shoved back on the creature looming large in his head.

"Fucking scum, that's what they are. Murdering scum." Trent's voice dropped a note or ten, filling with gravel.

Lorne could hardly sort out her scent from the land and the growing agitation from the lions. As soon as she neared, unassuming smile on her face, he hopped off Nova. The horse was the first line of defense, blocking the view as much as possible. He was the next, slamming to a halt on his side of the barbed wire. "Don't stop here."

Her eyebrows shot together and caution clouded her scent. Her eyes darted over his shoulder. The stink of fur and dominance hung heavy in the air, but it must have been Trent's growing growls that caught her attention.

Fuck. Last thing he needed was the lion bursting out of the man and taking a bite out of the human. Eating a SEA agent would be a sure way of eradicating the entire pride.

"Head toward the mountains. I'll catch up. Don't stop." He swallowed hard. "Sloan, go."

Miraculously, she wrenched the front end around and kicked the engine into action.

Lorne whipped back around to find Trent hunched over in his saddle, glaring murder at Sloan's back. Bright amber eyes smoothly switched to him, at odds with the bent body of his human half. Man and beast fought with one another, and he didn't need the sickly sweet scent of madness to tell him just how tenuously Trent held himself together.

His bear raged at him to let loose and put the crazed beast down. Mercy, it'd be. Ridding the world of a threat to his mate.

"Three percent. Don't fuck me over, Bennett," Trent snarled.

Lorne raised his hands slowly. "Three percent. Agreed."

He waited until the lions wheeled around before letting go of his breath. The air clearing of baked earth and fur soothed his bear just enough to focus on the trail leading away from Crowley territory and closer to Black Claw lands.

Sweet strawberries and cream called to him. He'd failed her before. Snapped at her and driven her away.

He needed to make amends.

The shiver that worked down his spine outed the lie he told himself. Amends, sure. Getting close enough to taste her, yes.

His bear rumbled approval and filled his head with more sendings of the tough woman bearing his mark on her skin.

Dead man, he reminded the beast. Breaking that conclusion would be a feat, especially if Ian and the rest of the Bennetts had progressed to forcing an animal on unsuspecting humans. Blood was his future, not a mate.

He unlatched the fencing between the Crowley and Ashford lands and closed it again, scratching at his beard with a growl in his throat. By the Broken. Just how far had the family fallen? He shouldn't have been surprised. Lilah barely escaped with her life. Him, too, for that matter.

He mounted Nova and loped in the direction he'd sent Sloan. The rumble of the ATV was still clear in his ears and grew louder as the mare closed the distance.

Then he spotted her, and the ache behind his eyes faded into nothing. Even the tightness of his shoulders relaxed and left him with just the memory of aching muscles.

Lorne rode up, thankful she wasn't pushing the machine to its fullest and impressed when she didn't startle at his appearance by her side.

As soon as the engine cut, he jerked his chin toward the empty range over her shoulder. "Where's your partner?"

She pointed to the radio on her hip. "Already

called in, so no throwing me over your shoulder and carrying me off like a caveman."

"Hm," he grunted. "You tell him you're working your source?"

"Might have." She planted her hands on her hips. "What was all that about?"

"Crowley pride doesn't take kindly to strangers. They like humans even less." He eyed her steadily. "He watched his family get butchered by hunters as a kid."

Sloan's mouth dropped open and her posturing slipped away in shock. "No. Tell me you're kidding."

"I wish I could say I was. You should probably warn your friends back at the office to steer clear of their fence line."

She nodded slowly, disgust still in her scent even though she'd wiped it from her face. "What were you doing out there?"

Lorne grunted. "Had to clean up some messes Alex and Hunter made."

"You do that a lot? Cleaning up other people's messes?"

He warded her off with a raised hand. "Only when it's people I care about. And only when they can't do it themselves."

She cocked her head with a tiny smile playing on her lips. He'd said something right, it seemed.

Her radio crackled, then a voice scratched between them. "Kent, report back. Any trouble?"

Sloan slanted the device close to her lips. "All good. Just a lesson in local preferences."

The other voice chuckled. "They sure have that. Head back this way. I'm starving."

"Be there shortly," she answered.

No. Too soon. Lorne's bear growled in his head and he swallowed back the noise. The voice over the radio wanted to steal her away before he got the chance to make his apologies.

Her eyes were already shutting him out. The bright, wide openness shifted her back from Sloan the Woman to Sloan the Agent. She had a job to do, which put him firmly on the other side of the fence.

Literally.

Lorne wanted to rip through the barbed wire just like he wanted to tear down the wall she was building between them. That started with making amends for acting like an ass.

He whipped off his Stetson and rubbed a hand over the back of his head before she could answer her partner. "I wanted to apologize for the other day."

"There are these magical devices, you know. Phones? They can reach just about anyone, anywhere."

He huffed a single breath of a laugh. Feisty woman. "I didn't know what to say."

"How about you start with the apology and segue into an explanation?" She shrugged. "We haven't found Ian yet, by the way. Maybe something you say could help."

Lorne frowned as he hopped off Nova and tied her reins to the fence post. He dug out an orange and pocket knife from a small pack hanging off the saddle horn, then ducked through the fence. He needed the extra time to put his words together.

"I meant when I said I wouldn't be an informant. Even if I knew where he was—and I don't—you shouldn't go anywhere near him."

"I'm not some damsel, Lorne. I can make up my own damn mind. This is my job. One family has already been hurt. Let me make sure there's not another."

Damsel in distress, never. She could hold her own. Right then, it was with fire in her eyes while she stared him down. Serving justice looked good on her.

He sliced through the orange and offered her a

piece, which she daintily pulled from the tip of the knife. His bear chuffed when she bite into the slice. Providing for her, that was the job of a good mate.

Lorne automatically pushed back on the images flashing through his head. The sendings from his bear were like living out another timeline. They'd only get stronger and harder to navigate with what was happening in his reality if he let himself consider that life as an option.

Mate, his bear insisted.

Not with Ian around.

"Things with Ian and the rest of my family are... difficult. They're rotten people with no love for outsiders. Like with Trent, humans catch the brunt of that. I got clear of them as soon as I could. I didn't want you to get caught up in them."

Still, he wanted to keep her. Selfish. Every second with him dragged her deeper into danger.

Blue eyes stared at him. After a moment, she cocked her head to the side. "I understand."

And she did. They weren't just words said to make him feel better. Zero hint of a lie swirled in her scent. Trouble resided in her gaze, but she left it unsaid.

Curious woman. He was again confronted with the utter need to learn everything about her. Hidden currents pushed her this way and that, just like they did to everyone else in the world. He wanted to dip into hers.

After picking out a seed and dropping it to the ground, she gestured around. "So this is your view from the office every day."

"Just about. Most days don't involve saving a lady from herself, though," he teased.

"Hah hah. Thanks for helping me avoid being used as a chew toy." She bit into another slice of orange he offered. "There's a rundown looking place I've passed a few times. Sometimes has trucks there, sometimes not. Can you tell me what it is, or is that some enclave secret?"

"Sounds like Defiant Dog. It's a rough bar for all us scoundrels on the edge of the territory. Not anywhere anyone decent should go."

"So naturally, you're there at least once a week?" Her brows arched with innocence, but her eyes glittered with mischief.

"Twice, if I'm lucky." His lips twitched at the corners. "The mates—Tansey and Joss—they like the bar in town better, so that's where we usually go these days."

"Good to know," Sloan mused.

Without missing a beat, he asked with a smirk,

"Planning to track me there, Agent?"

"Might have some follow-up questions for you," she answered just a little more airy than her previous responses.

A drop of juice rolled over the swell of her lip and down her chin.

Lorne reached out and caught up before it could drip onto her clothes. Electricity sang along his nerves the moment he touched her skin. Warmth spread up his palm and wrist and arm, and settled in the hollow of his chest.

Lorne brought his finger to his mouth and sucked the tiny drop of juice from his skin. Citrus mingled with the faintest taste of her.

Not enough. Never enough.

Her eyes widened in surprise, dilated pupils eating away at the bright blue color. Music pounded in his ears before he realized it was simply her pulse kicking up a notch.

The reaction confirmed he didn't just imagine her response to his touch. She felt it, too.

*Mate.*

*Bite. Mark.*

*Claim.*

He bent slowly, giving her time to retreat if she wanted. Her soft scent filled his nose and made his mouth water. He didn't want her to step back and put space between them.

He nearly groaned when she leaned forward to close the distance.

Lorne savored her taste exploding on his tongue. All the tumbling thoughts of pushing her away to save her vanished in the first sip. Another stroke of his tongue against hers pulled a growl from his chest and a muffled laugh from hers.

His bear rumbled happily. Kissing her, making her scent perk up with bubbly euphoria and arousal, that felt good. Felt right.

Felt too much like what he stood to lose.

Lorne eased back. Blue eyes fluttered open to watch him. Carefully, yes, but not a trace of shuttering.

"You should go before—" he cut off with a growl. Her hands tightened on his shirt and pulled him back down to her level.

"Before what?" she asked against his lips. "Before you apologize again?" She pecked him. "Before you kiss me again?" She nipped at him.

Another growl, and he claimed her mouth harder than before. He angled her face, hands cupping her cheeks. He stroked into her mouth rhythmically, matching her bite for bite, groan for groan. His cock swelled in his jeans and all he could think about was pulling her off her ATV and ripping her uniform down around her ankles. She'd joked about taking orders, and fuck, he wanted to give her some.

The radio crackled again. "Skies above, Kent, you better be dead. I'm not waiting on you much longer."

Sloan eased back and fixed him with narrowed eyes. "You're a bad influence," she grumbled, voice full of the smile she struggled to keep off her face.

Lorne smirked and nipped at her earlobe. "Duty calls."

She let loose a cleansing breath, then pressed a button on the radio. "Don't get hangry, Snow. I'm on my way." To him, she said, "Thanks for the snack."

By the Broken, he didn't want to let her go. He reached for anything to bring them back together. Danger or not, he couldn't rely on accidental meetings to hold him over. "Let me take you to the Summertime Fest. You want to learn about the people around here? Seeing them turn on the fun is how to do it."

She rose up enough to reach into her pocket and drew out a thin case that she popped open. A second later, she held a card between her fingers. "Here. In case you figure out how a phone works."

Sloan didn't even wait for a response before

settling back in her seat and starting the ATV up again.

Lorne was left with a business card, a tiny cloud of dust, and a sense that Sloan Kent would be the most challenging person who'd ever entered his life.

## CHAPTER 9

"Our next competitor comes from our own Black Claw Ranch. Lorne Bennett!"

Sloan sat up. A little further down and off to the side, the rest of the Black Claw clan also perked up in attention.

Well, mostly. Hunter wrapped an arm around Joss and wiggled his fingers against her ribs, which made her squirm. The sudden jump jostled Tansey, which spilled a tub of nacho chips onto the metal bleachers at their feet. Ethan growled over Tansey's head and Alex jammed an elbow into Hunter's side.

Sloan didn't have time for more than a quick smile. A buzzer sounded and a gate slammed open. Lorne shot out, pushing his horse hard. Clods of dirt were thrown into the air with the quick leaps forward as they raced toward the first barrel.

Sloan caught her breath. Both horse and rider leaned so far into the turn she thought they'd topple over. They circled, righted, then raced for a second, then a third, cutting so close on the last that Lorne raised his leg to avoid hitting the barrel itself. Circuit complete, he leaned low against his saddle and raced out the way he entered.

The announcer shouted stats and times which seemed to be impressive by the cheering of the crowd. Sloan pushed to her feet and made her way down the bleachers.

This was it. She'd agreed to meet Lorne after he competed. She wasn't particularly thrilled by the nervous jumble of butterflies tickling her stomach, but they didn't stop her from looking for him.

Or for anyone else that could be watching.

She hadn't received any other notes or proof of being stalked, but the idea of someone with a camera stayed in the back of her mind in all her interactions. So she used the same advice she'd given to victims. She changed up her routines, never taking the same roads home—hard in such a small town—or grabbing food at the same hour.

They wanted her scared. They wanted her questioning everything and to bow down under their threats.

Well, fuck them. Fuck Jimmy Culpepper. Fuck all his cronies. They watched her, but so what? They could see her getting on with her life without a single thought wasted on their shenanigans.

Then she spotted Lorne moving smoothly through the crowd. A smile lifted her lips as all her wariness fell away.

He'd changed since he raced through the arena. The tight, dark green t-shirt wasn't the long-sleeved, checkered one he'd worn during the competition. He'd washed himself down, too, smelling like fresh soap and sexy man.

He stooped and planted a quick kiss on her cheek, saving her from the awkwardness of deciding exactly how to greet him after being run off his ranch between two toe-curling kisses.

Even though her heart thundered in her chest, she played it cool with a shrug of one shoulder. "So this is what you country boys do for fun. I always pictured rodeos as just riding bulls."

"It's nothing big. Amateur hour, really. It's a women's event on the big circuit, but enough of us here race for bets or fun. Easier to set up some barrels than find some bucking stock." He wiped the back of his hand across his forehead, then settled his cowboy hat on his head. "But I like this better than traditional calf roping."

"I know some of those words," Sloan admitted with a small shake of her head. "I'll trust you on it being fun. Looked like a way to break your neck to me."

"Says the woman zipping around on her ATV. Bet more people die on those than horseback every year." He snorted, then eyed the crowd behind her. Something close to panic laced through his features and he quickly turned to press a hand against the small of her back. The little nudge got her moving. "Have you eaten yet? Been on any of the rides?"

Sloan shot a puzzled glance over her shoulder only to find the rest of the Black Claw clan staring at them both with mixtures of disbelief, awe, and confusion on their faces.

A sliver of hurt dug into her heart. Was he keeping her hidden from them? Embarrassed about stepping out with a human?

"Came here first," she said lightly. "Thought I'd watch you and then we'd figure out from there."

"In that case, let's head toward the middle of town."

He grabbed her hand, twining their fingers

together like he'd done it a thousand times before, and tugged her forward into a swirl of people.

Warmth heated her skin where they touched and zipped straight up her arm. In three steps, her entire body buzzed with yearning for the man. A single peck on the cheek and held hands weren't enough to quench her desire by a long shot.

And when he glanced down at her with dark eyes churning with a bit of gold, she nearly melted into a puddle.

He strode down the street slowly, and she got her first leisurely look at the Summertime Fest. Laughter spilled over from the town square filled with booths all advertising prizes for a game of chance. They passed basketballs for large stuffed animals, tossed rings for tiny goldfish, and even target practice for tickets.

When they hit the other side, her nose filled with delicious scents of carnival food. Hot, fried, greasy, and all making her stomach rumble with cravings.

What truly surprised her were the number of local signs instead of the metal trailers she'd seen at other fairs. She recognized the names of the town's restaurants—each with tables laden with their popular dishes. Outside of those were booths for a frozen lemonade stand manned by an elderly couple, donuts and other fried breads, and lots of words proclaiming ingredients fresh, homegrown, and local.

"What would you like?" Lorne rumbled at her side.

"Oh, I don't know. All of it?" she laughed.

His eyes danced at her. "How about we get some barbecue first? Then maybe an elephant ear or twelve."

"Don't forget the turkey legs and cotton candy."

"Woman, what do you think is for dinner?"

Sloan arched her eyebrows at him in mock surprise. "Oh, you think you're keeping me for that long? Mighty confident of you."

Lorne pulled her close with a rumbled growl. "At least until after dessert."

His breath tickled her ear, but his tone had her heart lodged in the back of her throat. Pure sex. His words dripped with promise that sparking over her skin.

It was almost a regret when he stepped away from her, but then he grabbed her hand and pulled her after him again.

With a tray piled with at least three complete meals for him, a sandwich combo for her, and beers for each of them, they made their way to an area with picnic tables. Kids begged parents to get their faces painted in the booth across the makeshift thoroughfare while street performers danced and sang in a routine.

"So. Initial thoughts on your first Bearden gathering?" Lorne asked.

"This is... different," she said after swallowing down her first bite. Her eyes nearly rolled to the back of her head. She'd had meals from Hogshead Joint before, but they'd outdone themselves.

"Different good?"

Nearby, two bear cubs wrestled hard enough to roll end over end into the walking path. Their father didn't skip a beat in his conversation with their mother. He simply grabbed them both by the scruff and set them on either side of him.

The crowd itself was as varied as the entertainment. Most of the shifted individuals had the look of juveniles, so she assumed they were children in their human forms. Bear cubs were the most common, but the odd wolf or big cat were also in attendance.

"My folks used to talk about entire blocks of the city shutting down for parties. Neighbors coming together and letting the kids run wild on summer days, fun and games. You know, the shit you see in movies idolizing the bygone era," she gestured dramatically. "But no one does that anymore. Everyone keeps to themselves. I don't think I ever met my neighbors the entire time I lived on my own in Atlanta. Closest to this was the few times we made it to the state fair. But even then, it was small groups keeping to themselves. While here..."

"Everyone knows each other."

"Yeah. Exactly. So we're eating here, together, but I've counted at least five people who nodded or lifted their fingers to you in greeting."

He had his place in the world. A clan to clean up after. Men who supported him no matter the trouble that showed up looking for him.

Sloan shrugged to scratch at the itch of feeling like an outsider. Human on the shifter squad, human in a shifter town. "So, different. Not sure how I feel about losing my anonymity. Especially when I am who I am."

"Agent Kent," he said without accusation.

"Agent Kent," Sloan agreed.

"To becoming Sloan." He raised his beer and clinked it with hers. "You're here, no uniform, chowing down on the same pulled pork that they all eat at least once a month. It's not an overnight change, but it's something."

"That easy?"

"Not easy, no," he grunted. "Took me years and I still don't feel part of them sometimes."

"Does that ever make you want to pack up and leave? Start fresh somewhere else?"

He looked out over the crowd of shifters and humans and whoever else mingled in with the press of bodies. "No," he said finally. "I don't want to give this place up."

She was beginning to feel the same.

After they finished eating, he led her toward the booths filled with arts and crafts. The real, true Bearden, he described them. And like the food court staffed by a majority of local options, the people of Bearden had their own items to sell. Everything from wood carvings to paintings of the landscape to freshly potted plants—both decorative and consumable—were available for anyone interested.

The town was lively, she could see that. And just like any other population she'd encountered. So what if they had some extra power in their blood, or growled a little more, or needed a fresh, consenting vein to survive? They still needed to eat and drink, still tried to make the world beautiful, and still wanted to party.

"And there's something like this multiple times a

year?" Sloan asked as the afternoon slid toward evening.

Space at one end of the town square cleared out and a crew hauled musical gear into the gazebo. They even joined wood boards together to construct a dance floor over the grass.

"About once a month, give or take. Not nearly this big. This is one of the major festivals. Firsts usually get some—first calves born, first rain, first snow. Graduations. Any excuse to stop the town for the day and get together, they take it."

They were crazy. In a good way.

"Fireworks display tonight." He bumped her shoulder. "If you're into that."

"Mmm. What trouble are you planning under the cover of darkness?"

A wicked smile hitched up one corner of his mouth. "Oh, all kinds."

Lorne pulled her close. All the light touches and heated glances culminated in that breath of a moment, right before he bent his face to hers. Gold eyes caught hers, looking for any sign of resistance or hesitation. He sipped at her lips gently, taking his time to reacquaint himself with her. Sloan balled her fists in his shirt and steadied herself against him.

He felt more real than the few men that professed

to love her. How quickly she'd grown comfortable with him. Maybe because they'd done away with any idea of him being an informant. He'd taken on the role of a friend.

A very hot, very available friend.

He was quieter than most men she'd been with. Mysterious. But attentive and caring. He didn't seem the slightest bit bothered that she carried a gun to work. Probably because he was half-beast himself and didn't need to worry about being manhandled by a girl.

Lorne pulled back suddenly, nostrils flaring and entire body going stiff. Sloan glanced up, only to find him glaring over the top of her head. She whirled around and tried to find what distracted him.

There.

She recognized the face before he turned away.

Ian Bennett.

Lorne stared after him. "I need to take care of something," he muttered.

"I'm going with you."

"Sloan, you need to stay out of this. It has nothing to do with you."

The order grated on her. Sloan narrowed her

eyes. "Well, we either go together, or I follow you. Your choice."

Lorne growled, but nodded. Without another response, he pushed through the crowd and after Ian.

They followed him through the stalls of food and games, though he seemed to have a destination in mind and didn't try to throw their tail. If anything, the pauses and sly looks over his shoulder were making sure he was noticed.

The hair on the back of her neck raised with uncertainty the moment they spotted Ian pass through the door of The Roost.

Lorne didn't pause and didn't notice her hitched step. Sloan quickly ran down a mental list of who worked extra security that day, then typed out a message and sent it to August. She just had to keep eyes on the man until backup arrived. She had no way to contain him herself if he put up a fuss. Silver cuffs and her badge had been left at home.

Stay out of it? Not when a family had already been hurt. Not when the man possibly responsible was seated at the town's main bar, looking smug as hell.

Ian threw his arms wide as soon as they pushed through the door. "What, no hello for your cousin?"

Their steps sounded loud as they crossed over the wooden floorboards. The place was empty save for a few faces, most everyone electing to spend their boozing time out in the fair. A lone man stood guard at the bar, black hair mussed and fiery eyes carefully watching Ian.

"You never should have come here, Ian," Lorne said almost sadly.

"Never should have done a lot of things, you know that. But here we are. Ain't no changing the past."

Sloan quirked an eyebrow and tried to parse the conversation. Layers of history existed between the men. She could almost smell the animosity.

"You banging this one?" Ian pointed at her with the mouth of his bottle. "You always had a thing for humans."

"Leave her out of this." The tinge of sadness left Lorne's voice until only a deep, gravelly growl exited his lips.

As much as she appreciated the sentiment, the words raised her hackles. Sloan shifted from foot to foot and glowered at both men. She didn't need Lorne's protection.

Ian shrugged, wolfish smile on his face. "No matter. We drove one off before. We can do it again."

"No."

"What? You're not picking her, are you? Over your own flesh and blood?" Ian poked a hard finger into Lorne's chest. "You're a Bennett. You belong with us."

Lorne slapped away Ian's hand. "I haven't been one of you in years. You need to get out of here, Ian. You never should have tried to find me."

"Yeah, you keep saying that." Ian pushed to his feet. They were nearly the same height. Same dark hair, same dark eyes. Both flashed with gold at that moment. "We have unfinished business."

The air felt heavy. Nothing changed that she could see or hear, but goose bumps rose up and down her arms. Even her heart struggled to beat under the weight of whatever pressed down upon the room.

Her fingers twitched to find any kind of weapon. A fight was coming. She could feel it in her bones.

August and Crewe stepped through the door, their shift on duty marked by the uniforms they wore and the serious looks on their faces as they zeroed in on the little party. They looked like twins, giving her the tiniest of nods.

The air didn't change. If anything, the press worsened.

Crewe and August sauntered over, one blocking an easy path to the door with a smooth lean against the bar.

"Ian Bennett, you need to come with us," Crewe said softly.

"What the fuck for?" Ian demanded loudly.

So much for not making a scene.

Lorne whipped around to her. Anger coated his expression. For Ian or for her, she wasn't sure.

"What did you do?" he growled.

She lifted her chin defiantly. "My job."

"We have some questions for you," August answered smoothly. "Don't make this more difficult on yourself."

"Difficult? You fuckers don't have the right to take me anywhere."

Crewe looked bored. "Sir, if you don't come peacefully, we'll be forced to remove you."

"Fucking traitors. You like sucking the dick of Big Government? Do you know what they consider us? Expendable."

"Like that poor bastard you bit into?"

Ian grinned. "Not anymore."

"Shit, that sound like a confession to you?" August asked.

"Sounds like it to me." Crewe grabbed Ian by the collar. "Ian Bennett, you're taking a ride with us."

"He's my problem," Lorne spat out, still focused on her.

Sloan slid between him and the others. She pressed a hand to his chest and flung his words back in his face. "Stay out of it."

Lorne turned cold eyes on her. "He needs to be put down," he said between gritted teeth.

"Same as you, cousin!" Ian shouted over his shoulder. August and Crewe marched him through the door.

Sloan took a step back from Lorne, feeling like she'd been slapped. "Is that what you planned to do with him?"

"If he couldn't be made to see reason." Lorne stared down his nose at her. "You're not like us. You don't understand. When an animal goes rabid, the only option is to kill it before it kills someone else."

Hatred whipped off him and socked Sloan in the gut. Dangerous man, that was Lorne. He kept up a careful exterior, but there was darkness inside him when the mask slipped.

"What happened between you two?" she asked on a breath.

"Enough that you should stay away."

On top of all her problems, the assholes that made her move, the ones who still wanted to make her miserable, she had to learn that her one bit of solace wasn't even that. Lorne had a past, too, and one that didn't seem all that savory.

Unfinished business, Ian said. Drove one off before.

The words scratched at the back of her mind. Outsider, that was all she'd ever be.

Lorne wanted to play at showing her around, but that was all it was—play. Because when it came down to it, he was just another shifter protecting his own. They didn't believe in the same kind of justice. She was too human, and he was too much a shifter.

Sloan took a step away from him. Then another. Something ripped apart inside her the more distance she put between them.

Necessary.

"You know where to find him," she said over her shoulder as she followed August and Crewe out the door.

She had a suspect to question.

# CHAPTER 10

Lorne laced his fingers behind his neck and watched the whirlwind blow through his life and leave him with nothing.

One minute, and he'd been having the time of his life. The next, and his family ripped him apart all over again.

The Bennett clan hadn't forgotten about him, that much was clear from the words that dripped out of Ian's mouth. Not that he had hope for anything else. They held fast to their grudges. They lived by their martyr complexes. When they needed a convenient sacrificial lamb, he was there to be slaughtered.

Unfinished business. Yeah, there was that. And now Ian knew who Sloan was, even rode in the same vehicle as her. He'd inhale her scent, learn all the fine notes, and track her down when it came time to do away with the threat.

Just like he and the others had done with Lilah.

Lorne growled and banished the sick and sour remembered scent of her fear from his mind. Lilah hadn't deserved any of the harm they'd visited upon her. But like Sloan, he'd been the one to put her in their sights.

His fists tightened at his sides. He'd killed once before to save the life of an innocent. He wasn't above doing it again, much as it'd tear the remaining good pieces of himself apart. He wasn't destined to live a whole or happy life. Fate had other plans for him, it seemed.

And Sloan. Tough, stubborn, gorgeous Sloan. She didn't understand his world. She put too much faith in her human systems of law and order. They were animals. Territorial beasts with laws of their own.

She'd be better off without him. He wouldn't let any of his family foam at the mouth near her.

He didn't want her tears to follow him to the grave.

Best if he cut ties and let her retreating back be the last he saw of her.

His head pounded with a sudden ache behind his

eyes. His bear pushed forward, slicing and chomping at him to let go of his control.

Lorne pressed his hands to his stomach and took a deep breath. It didn't help in the slightest.

His inner beast won out and forced a fresh round of sendings through his head.

Sloan, happy. Sloan, with laughs just for him. Sloan, with a scar on her shoulder proclaiming she was mated.

He'd accepted his lot in life before she barreled into him. He'd been prepared to face his fate. Now, though, his bear wasn't so willing to roll over and call it quits.

One final scene pushed through. Blood covered him. Ian's body lay at his feet.

Fight back, was the sentiment.

Head still feeling like he'd pressed himself between a vice, Lorne stomped off toward the area set aside for the rodeo competition. His skin felt too tight and his shoulders were solid masses of muscle that wouldn't give. He wanted to shift. He wanted to get the fuck away from all the people that had descended on Bearden.

He silently swore when he caught sight of the clan huddled together, almost like they knew exactly where to be to cause him more trouble. Joss held a stuffed bear as large as herself. Ethan and Tansey picked at a stick of pink and blue cotton candy. Jesse, Hunter, and Alex nursed beers and shot the shit.

Every last one of them turned worried eyes on him as he blasted forward.

"Where have you been?" Alex grumbled. "You missed the awards."

Awards? Fuck awards. He didn't give a shit about a shiny trophy when the rest of his world was black and dull. He'd agreed to compete after hours of badgering and before Ian showed his ugly mug. He'd gone through with it when he had solid plans to meet up with Sloan.

Now it all seemed so... worthless.

Lorne blew past the group. He needed to collect his horse and get back to the ranch, maybe out of town. Put as much distance as he could between himself and Sloan. Draw Ian and any other Bennetts away.

"Was that her? The one?" Tansey demanded as she stumbled after him, struggling to keep pace.

Lorne grunted.

The one. His idiot bear liked the sound of those words. His human half knew better.

"Where is she now?" Joss asked softly.

The question stopped them in their tracks. Pity clouded their collective scent.

"Lorne, slow it down a minute," Jesse rumbled. He went so far as to reach for him, brushing a palm over his shoulder.

Lorne jerked out of the touch and made a beeline for the competitors' horses. He didn't want, or need, any of their reassuring touches, dammit. He just needed to be alone.

Nova nickered softly when he opened the makeshift stall door. Her ears flicked in all directions as he led her out and used her big body to block off the questions fired at him. He twisted the lock on the horse trailer and let down the ramp, then led her inside.

He turned to head back and collect the rest of his tack, but found Hunter already there with saddle and blankets in hand. Those found their place in the trailer and he shut the door with a thud.

"Give him space," Tansey muttered somewhere in the background.

Smart woman. No wonder she'd snagged Ethan's eye. She had to be on the lookout for any danger that came for their clan.

Right that moment, danger radiated off Lorne.

His bear prowled just under the surface, waiting to lash out.

In silence, he slid behind the steering wheel of his truck and turned the engine over. He needed to disappear.

Lorne shook hard by the time he whipped around the final bend of the ranch road and pulled up to the barn. Whatever his problem, he owed it to the innocent creature in the trailer to get her home. She wasn't responsible for any of the tightness in his chest.

Nova whinnied as soon as he ripped open the back of the trailer and urged her down the ramp. Other horses peeked over the edges of their stalls when he led her through the doors and settled her in her place. With a final pat on the neck, Lorne turned and slipped back into the night.

The skies were clear, which felt unfair. He wanted storms and winds whipping around him in a violent tempest. He wanted something outward to reflect the turmoil within him.

Lorne let his bear have his skin. Pops and cracks tore his human shape apart and reformed him into something wild. Fur slid out of his pores and settled in a thick coat along newly formed limbs. Claws cut into the earth, curved and ready for action.

Except he had no one to fight but himself.

Lorne growled into the darkness, and ran.

Time faded into nothing as he plowed forward. Across the ranch, off Black Claw territory, he ran until he hit the river and turned further into the mountains. He needed the scent of woods and trees around him. They smelled nothing like the dust of home and he wanted as little reminder as possible of those horrid years.

Minutes, hours, he wasn't sure. Colored lights bloomed and died in the sky, but now only the moon and stars broke up the darkness. When the agitation coursing through him faded to a dull buzz, he stopped along the river. Spray from the waterfall created a light mist right where the stream drove into the mirrored surface. Above, near the halfway point, a small bridge crossed in front of the falls. Townsfolk and tourists alike loved the spot.

Lorne loved it when it was empty. This was his spot when he needed peace from everyone.

Right then, he had plans to make. He never should have left the homestead. Never should have kissed Sloan. Never should have taken up with Lilah in the first place.

The family was gunning for him. He needed to make sure no one else got hurt. Bennetts took care of their own. Those words were ingrained in him from a young age. He just never expected them to mean death.

Noise to his left forced him to lift his head. A growl of warning entered the air to ward off the intruder.

He was almost disappointed when he recognized Hunter's outline instead of Ian's. He wanted the fight. He wanted an end to the waiting.

Hunter took a seat next to him and planted a cold beer in the dirt right next to a bundle of clothes. "I'm not leaving, so you either sit there like a big dumb animal, or shift and share a drink with me."

Lorne lifted a lip and snarled.

Hunter shrugged like his threats didn't matter. Lorne wanted to show him how serious he was with claws and fangs.

Except... not really. The man was a jerk half the time and an idiot the other half. He also saw more than he let on. He couldn't keep his mouth shut, but he let the clown facade hide him from any true responsibility. That was something Lorne understood. Walls and barriers came easily to him.

Hunter took a long draw from his bottle and stared out over the water. Moonlight filtered through the trees and reflected off the surface. The scene would have been peaceful without the irritated growl that rumbled in Lorne's chest.

Interloper. He wanted to be alone.

Hunter didn't look at him when he finally spoke. "You had the mates in a tizzy with your smooth exit."

Not his problem. They had someone to run to for comfort. Unlike him.

"I'm sure Ethan will release you if you want. It'd suck to lose you, but he's not an alpha to hold you against your will. You could go to the lions, or skip town."

Lorne let his shift ripple through him slowly. He wanted the pain.

"Ethan isn't the problem," he rasped.

"Is it us, then? I know Alex is a shithead and Jesse secretly wants us to hug and roast marshmallows together, but they aren't so bad."

Hunter's tone stayed light, but a strand of hurt entered his scent.

Lorne eyed the man while he stuffed himself into the jeans he'd brought. He'd thought of them as clan in only the most distant sense. He was pledged to Ethan, he tolerated the others, he worked to make sure they didn't murder each other. But actually getting close? He'd done his best to keep a distance. Dead men didn't have futures.

The thin tinge of pain told a different story. He might have held back, but someone else looked to him as a friend.

Lorne sat back down with a scowl. "It's not any of you," he admitted. He picked at the label on his bottle and mulled his words. "There's shit from the past coming back on me now. I'm not safe for anyone to be around."

"You know, when things were going tits up with Joss, my old man pushed his words on me. And for once in that old codger's life, they were actually as profound as he made them out to be." When Lorne didn't respond, Hunter continued. "Be there. Show up. Hold on until the very last second. If you're lucky, you'll dodge the stomping hooves of life. Because it's important to stay with it when you find a real connection. For people like us, they don't come very often."

"Pretty words." Lorne shrugged. "Reality isn't like the fairy tales. Sometimes the villains win."

"So you'll, what? Give up?" Hunter snorted. "Fuck that. If you want this girl, make the ground red with blood and fight off everyone standing in your way. You know we'll have your back."

"For an agent who was ready to keep you locked

up while they took down the people holding your mate captive?"

"No. For *your* mate." Hunter waved a hand. "Oh, don't look so shocked. Could only be one thing to make you this much of an idiot."

"Yeah. Having it spread from you." Lorne scratched at his beard.

"Only thing spreading from me is wisdom gained through years of being right."

"Wisdom gained from dumbass mistakes." A ghost of a smile hitched up Lorne's lips.

"Truth speaker." Hunter canted his head. "Come on. Let me give you a lift home. Joss will skin me alive if I let you stay out here all night."

Lorne stayed seated a moment longer.

He'd had trouble putting his feet into motion and getting clear of the men from Black Claw. He'd justified it to himself as keeping them steady, or a lack of threats staring him down. Even when he decided he had to leave, he'd still been unable to actually do it.

Hunter was right about one thing. For whatever reason, he'd hung on tight to his clan. They were his people. Idiots, all of them. Crazier than him. But still good. With the rejection of one family came the acceptance of another.

He had a place among the Black Claw clan.

A piece of himself, rusty and bent out of shape, slid into position. Others still poked into him, slashed at him, burned him wherever he brushed against them. Work to be done. Fixes to be made. Nothing came easy.

But he had to try.

Not just with the clan, either. He'd drawn the line between himself and everyone else for so long, telling himself he did it to keep them safe, he wasn't sure how to let someone in. Wanting to be otherwise wasn't enough. He had to figure out the pieces and put them together.

Lorne pushed to his feet and followed Hunter out of the woods.

# CHAPTER 11

Sloan glared at Ian through the glass. He smirked back as if he knew exactly where she stood. He didn't, she knew, but she couldn't shake the feeling that those cold eyes were focused on her.

"You didn't need to come in," August said at her side. "We had it under control."

"I know. I wanted to hear what he had to say."

She'd stayed with August and Crewe the entire night. Useless, but she couldn't pull herself away. Even as Ian pissed and moaned about his violated rights, she stayed. When he fell silent, she didn't leave. They'd tried waiting him out, all three entering at separate times to ask their questions, but the man hadn't said a word in response.

When dawn struck, he finally uttered the dreaded word. "Lawyer."

The lawyer had arrived not even an hour after placing the call and looked as weaselly as they came. Slicked back hair and eyes that darted around the room, he infuriated everyone as soon as he called agents back into the room.

"My client intends to cooperate fully. With regards to your ridiculous line of questions, he can give you his exact location on the day of the attack. Right down to the hour, I'm told."

"Gas receipts. I went in to pay with cash. You can probably check the security cameras. I wasn't anywhere near that campground," Ian stated.

Sloan wanted to punch the smirk off his fucking face.

August turned from the glass with a disgusted tick in his throat. "Did you need to hear all that because of your new boyfriend?"

"He's not my boyfriend," she grumbled.

"Yeah? That why you smell like him?" Her partner waved a hand. "Better be careful. You might find yourself invited to Sunday dinner with me and the mate."

Sloan rolled her eyes. "Fuck off. We both know

you eat at a trough and no woman would allow you at her table."

Inside the box, Crewe cocked his head to the side. "So if you weren't anywhere near the campground, do you have any idea who was? Because our witness statements put you there. You have a twin, Mr. Bennett? Some other relative looking exactly like you?"

"The one and only," Ian answered in a smarmy tone.

Nothing else exited his mouth. Crewe went back and forth with him, prodded for anything incriminating or a new lead, but Ian gave up nothing.

Asshole. He might not have hurt this particular family, but Sloan was certain he had a hand in others. Lorne called his entire family bad news, and the layered talk between them scratched at her instincts. She memorized Ian's face. No doubt, she'd see it again someday.

Crossed arms and glares greeted Ian when he was finally released from the interrogation room. More than a few agents shifted uncomfortably when he stretched his arms out wide and rolled his shoulders, making a display of his regained freedom. His lawyer whispered something Sloan didn't catch, but the nearest shifters did. Rolled eyes and looks of disgust followed him to the elevator.

"Well, that was a bust," Crewe announced once the doors dinged closed and left the agents alone. "Motherfucker had a solid alibi and doesn't even smell like he's lying. We're back to square one."

Frustrated sighs rolled through the room with the news. Work the case, that was all they could do. They had it easy. Some poor man was laid up in a quarantine facility until he could find a bear clan to sponsor him and ease his transition into shifter life.

The elevator dinged open again. "Whoa, excuse me. Coming through."

The voice raised alarm in the ranks. Uncertainty rippled through them and spread out until all eyes were fixed on the redhead wobbling in their center and trying to peer around the pile of boxes in her hand.

Crewe poked his head out of his office at the disturbance. "Ms. Warren, how did you get back here?"

"Oh, a nice pair of men came out as I was coming in. They held the door for me." With a sigh, Joss Warren dropped the boxes on the nearest desk, shoving aside a stapler and toppling a pen cup in the process. Neither of which seemed to register.

"You can't just waltz in here," Crewe tried again.

"I brought cookies!" she exclaimed in a sing-song voice. "And brownies, too! Chocolate chip, peanut butter, I think there might even be some fudge in one of these." She pried open one lid, then shifted the order of the boxes. Two more, and she held the box aloft. "A-ha! White chocolate, raspberry ripple. Who wants it?"

The silence weighed over the room while red crept up Crewe's neck.

Sloan stepped in before he could explode at the woman. Her people were just one misstep after another. But she'd brought treats, so whatever the true reason for her visit, at least there was a hit of sugar waiting at the end.

"It's okay, Crewe. I got her."

He turned gold eyes on her. "Make it quick."

"Come on," Sloan said. She jerked a thumb over her shoulder. "This way."

Joss took a step forward, then whirled around and gestured to the boxes. "Dig in, please! They're my gift and giant thank you for helping out with that *tiny* little problem a few weeks ago."

Joss stumbled to her side and whispered loudly. "I was hoping to get you alone." She bit back her laugh. "Sloan, alone. It rhymes."

Sloan resisted passing a hand over her face.

She led Joss into the break room and offered to pour a cup of coffee. Joss nodded gratefully and doctored hers with a spoonful of sugar.

Seated at a table, Sloan fixed her with a steady gaze. "What are you doing here?"

"Hoooonestly?" Joss ducked her gaze. "I wanted to make sure there were no hard feelings about Hunter's meddling. But really, it's to hide mine and Hunter's meddling with Lorne. And you, too."

Her eyes grew big, like she'd just realized what came out of her mouth. She raised her hands and shook them from side to side. "Please, please don't hold that against us. Me. Hold it against me. Don't, that is."

"Joss." Sloan pressed her lips together to keep from laughing. The woman was one-hundred percent unadulterated awkward truthfulness.

"We're just really excited and in love. When you know, you know. And I think you know about Lorne, and he definitely seems to know about you, even if he's grunting more than usual and refuses to talk about anything that's happening. We just want everyone to be as happy as us." A huge smile spread across her face.

That infectious smile tugged at Sloan's heart.

This woman, bound and held against her will by people wanting to do her great harm, wasn't wallowing in any of that. She had her place in the world, and it was at the side of a man willing to get into huge amounts of trouble to save her.

"You and Hunter," Sloan said flatly.

"Yes, exactly. We're just trying to spread love around like fat little cupids. But not those creepy babies. Or the adults in diapers. Cherubs! We're cherubs, dangit!"

Love. Hah! She might have had an intense desire to ride that cowboy, but love? Love was so far from her mind that it might as well not exist. Cherubs be damned.

Besides, he was cut from the same cloth as Ian and most of the other shifters she knew. Insular, the lot of them. Protective of their own. He didn't want her doing her job when it infringed on his life. That wasn't something she would sign up for in a partner.

"So that's why you brought a bunch of sweets. To act like not-creepy cupids."

Joss hesitated, then blazed on with her mission. "I just don't want you to give up on him. Not so soon. And I think that's what's going on with the way he stormed off last night. Hunter wasn't very forthcoming with what they talked about, but he was grumpy as heck and muttering up a storm about stubborn so-and-sos keeping him out and away from his mate at an unholy hour. But he had this little smile on his face, so I think it was promising, whatever was said."

"And listen," she continued before Sloan could finish processing her rapid-fire words, "he's got some issues, just like we all do. And sure, he's fluent in grunts and narrowed looks, but I don't think I've seen him so... at peace since I got here. Which is a not-small deal. These Black Claw boys love them some manly misery."

Sloan crossed her arms over her chest. "I'm not responsible for someone else's peace."

Especially when she couldn't trust he would have her back.

"No, you're not. You're right. But there's a balance, you know? That push and pull. The right person can make you better while you do the same for him."

"And you think Lorne is that someone?"

Joss shook her head and hands at the same time. "I'm not making that call. I'm just here to suggest you don't give up so quick. If you want. No pressure. But... what do you have to lose?"

Sloan stayed quiet. The answer was a big fat

nothing. She was already alone. She'd barely made headway with the new unit. Her old partner was as dirty as could be and his cronies wanted to erase her from history. Hosing off a cowboy in the midst of a wallow wasn't going to bring her any lower.

But would it help her up?

"So, I know this is probably sudden, but I want to ask you out on a date. A lady date. With Tansey."

Sloan stared at her until she squirmed.

"It's fun, I swear! We kick the guys out and put up these signs saying boys aren't allowed, like all those jerks did when we were kids and denied us use of their clubhouses. They're even laminated now, which makes it totally official." Joss drew in a breath and then rushed on. "And then we watch a movie and paint our nails and freaking bond like the badass bitches we are. Tansey's words, not mine. But I kind of like how they taste."

Joss won and Sloan couldn't keep the smile off her face. "No promises. To either thing. But I'll think on both."

The woman clasped her hands together under her chin and blinked green eyes watery with hope and enthusiasm. "That's all I ask!"

CHAPTER 12

Lorne followed the noisy clan up the stairs of Hogshead Joint. The scent of barbecue made his mouth water and his bear rumble in the back of his head. A little slice of heaven waited to be served up for their enjoyment.

And maybe he wasn't displeased with the company. After Hunter's pep talk, Lorne had sensed a hint of calm anticipation in his bear. Not peace, exactly. But hope that they were on the right path.

Lorne still didn't know what steps he needed to take to get there, but at least the beast wasn't slashing at his middle or trying to eat him from the inside out anymore. He celebrated the win.

Hunter and Alex jostled to reach the door first. Alex growled and Hunter bared his teeth in a vicious smile when their fingers wrapped around the handle at the same time.

"Would you two cut it out? We don't need another public brawl." Ethan made a noise in the back of his throat. He waded between them, air thickening with the pulse of power as he yanked open the door and guided Tansey through. "We're lucky Trent didn't use it as an excuse to pull his horses."

Lorne ducked his head and didn't say a word.

"Too bad. Could have used the time off," Alex muttered.

Jesse swatted him on the back of his head. "Like you even help with the rides, fucker."

"Which leaves me running everything else while you're off playing tour guide. A man can only do so much."

"Sounds fair to me. Can't rotate you in to handle the rides, so you're working where you won't bite someone."

Alex's snapped answer didn't register to Lorne. He followed the others to a long table in the corner and blindly placed his order for a bottle of beer.

One scent stood out to him. He followed the trail with his eyes.

Ian sat at the bar, slowly sipping at his beer and

watching a game play on the television. That he was there meant Sloan and her people must have come up with nothing. Lorne wasn't sure if he was glad or upset by that.

Still, not a good sign he hadn't left town. He wanted no part of Ian's unfinished business. He'd lived for too long expecting the shadow of death to fall over him. There hadn't been a reason to fight his fate. He'd killed, and he expected to be killed.

Not anymore.

Lorne glared at his cousin. How many times had they played in the pond on the Bennett property? How many sleepovers with the entire pack of boys piled on top of each other? They'd been so close, then. Loyal. No one ever said a bad word about the others, much to the annoyance of their parents. It'd finally come down to punishments for them as a group. Even with the noses to sniff out who lied, no one would go against their brothers or cousins.

Family, his father used to say with a shrug. That was what counted. Blood over everything else.

Those were the words repeated when they were swatted for covering for each other. The same words were repeated as warning against any involvement with humans. No good came from those people.

Couldn't he see that? Hadn't the clan suffered enough for the causes of humans?

Nods of agreement and grunts of suppressed emotion always answered the question. Having a furry side in the ranks of soldiers didn't mean discharge. No, it meant an even bigger helping of shit in an already traumatic and deadly war. The Bennett boys were raised on tales of jungle ambushes and traps laid to maim and dismember, but not to kill. Those that survived came back ready to keep on fighting the ones that sent them to into violence.

Humans weren't to be trusted. They were to be avoided, until the time came for them to be killed.

Lorne sucked down a ragged breath. Then came the years of school and sweethearts and growing up. They still had each other's backs.

Until they didn't.

Lorne always thought of senior prom as the moment his world went wrong, but cracks had appeared in the months leading up to that night.

He'd asked, Lilah accepted. None of Bennett boys were supposed to be there. He thought he'd be safe.

He was wrong.

Ian showed, with two of their cousins. Lorne didn't spot them until the end of the dances, just after he'd kissed Lilah in the middle of the damn room. Surrounded by humans.

They'd found her easily the following day. A kind word and offer to drive her out to meet him had been her undoing. Lorne showed up at her house shortly after for their date, but he'd been too late.

He knew exactly where they'd taken her. Where else would they have gone to send a message? Of course it was to their old clubhouse. A tree house on the ground, built from bits of junk and pieces of wood. It'd been their palace, and it became Lilah's terror.

Lorne's fingers tightened around his bottle as he remembered the screams of panic. They tormented her with what they were and what he was. Shifting from human to bear and back again, laughing when she showed shock and tried to run. That'd been a game in itself, seeing how far the little human could get before the bears rode down on her and smacked her feet out from under her.

His only solace was that the games never went any further. Maybe they had plans for it, he didn't know.

He could still remember Lilah's voice breaking when she said his name from the doorway. Blood covered his snout, and more marked his fur from the injuries they gave him. The body of his own damn brother at his feet should have ripped his heart apart, but the fear and pain in Lilah's voice always hit him harder in the gut.

He killed, but he destroyed her.

Lorne pushed to his feet and crossed through the restaurant, settling his Stetson on his head as he went. No more. He'd left that life behind long before he fought to save a human. He wouldn't be intimidated by a ghost from his past.

"You need to get out of town."

Ian slid him a glance, then went back to watching the game. "Why? Your girlfriend ain't going to do shit."

"Maybe, maybe not." He let his bear push forward enough to enter his eyes. "But it's me you have to worry about."

An infuriating smile curled up Ian's lips. "You and me, we have unfinished business."

"No. That business ended years ago. I moved on. You should, too."

Ian grabbed the collar of his shirt and yanked him close. "We're blood, Lorne. There's no undoing that."

Lorne curled his own fingers around Ian's fist and pressed hard on the soft parts of his wrist. His bear roared for more, demanding blood and death for the trouble Ian raised. "And yet, you're the only one here. Where are the others, Ian? Why aren't they backing you up right now?"

Something uncertain flickered in his cousin's eyes. Ian was alone. By his own doing or some other reason or even just temporarily, Lorne didn't care. Hell, he'd probably have felt sorry for the man if he hadn't started off with threats at their first words in years. He ruined any hope of a peaceful reunion with talk of the *unfinished business* between them.

Lorne struck at that weakness. "You see all those people I'm with? Every last one of them would help drag your body somewhere it won't be found."

"They aren't the only ones who know how to make someone disappear," Ian growled.

The threat was clear, and one neither Lorne nor his bear could abide.

A snarl rattled in his chest as he locked eyes with his cousin. Blood and gore were heavy in the sendings pushed at him from the beast. Lorne clung to control by a fingernail.

They used to be so close, and Lorne wouldn't shed a tear if he had to kill the man to keep Sloan safe.

Ian met him glare for glare. A sneer spread over his expression.

Lorne clamped down harder. "We share blood, cousin. We were raised on the same lessons. If you don't leave this town, I won't make it fast like Frank. I will have you begging for that final release. This is your warning. Leave."

Then he walked away.

His bear snarled for blood, for a fight, for anything other than making his way back to his clan and taking a seat at the very edge of the table. He drummed his fingers against the surface to keep from jamming sharpened claws into the wood.

Ian had his warning. More than he deserved, but Lorne didn't want to sink back into the sickness of the Bennett clan. He had his own people now. He had reasons to be better.

But he wouldn't shy from the fight if Ian wanted blood.

He tracked his cousin from his seat and out the door. Not a single ounce of relief touched him. He glowered in Hunter's direction. Something was supposed to change.

He felt exactly the same.

Lorne swallowed the last of his beer, then waved down the waitress for another while the sounds of happy couples and friends pressed on him hard enough to make his ears pop.

Back at the bar, Sloan stepped up to the pickup area for to-go orders.

Human in a shifter town, working a thankless job. One he hadn't respected when it came between him and running off his no-good relative. Her shoulders stayed stiff as if she expected there to be whispers about her and didn't want to show any weakness.

Her appearance was too big a stroke of luck. Fate was hell on a man. He wanted to get his life in order and clear any obstructions from the path before attempting to bring anyone on it with him. Ian was still spouting off his veiled threats. The time wasn't right.

Except when he glanced down the table, Hunter waggled his eyebrows up and down like he was trying to communicate in freaking Morse code.

Then Joss jammed an elbow to Hunter's side. "I saw it first."

"You? No way! I'm like a bloodhound for the potential for true love," Hunter sniped back.

"The only thing you have a nose for is the worst possible decisions," Joss yelled in a whisper.

Hunter leaned in quick and pecked her on the lips. "I know. You're the worst."

Lorne shook his head and stood before they started pushing plates and glasses out of the way to make the entire table witness to an inappropriate amount of affection. Even the glances his way were enough notice. He didn't need an audience for his next steps.

Which were...?

He scrubbed his hands against his jeans and blew out a harsh breath. His bear still rode him harshly for the denial of Ian's blood. The strawberries and cream of Sloan's scent calmed him, barely, and filled him with a mess of other desires.

*Mate.*

He wanted her. He just didn't know how to have her.

She'd be better off without him. He was a murderer by most standards, an outlaw by some. Too rough for a woman with a strong sense of right and wrong.

But the thought of her moving on or making a life with anyone else made his stomach roil and his bear roar.

*Mine.*

Lorne sidled up next to her and leaned against the bar. "Agent."

She started, then straightened, eyes shuttering her true expression. Wariness still clouded her scent. "Lorne," she said primly.

"Couldn't get enough the other day?" he asked in a light voice.

She arched a single eyebrow at him and said nothing.

He took off his Stetson and settled it on the bar. He ran a hand through his hair and winced. "I don't know how to do this."

"What? Pick up your order? You wait in line and pay, preferably without bothering anyone else," she snapped.

"No," he said softly. "Apologize."

She blinked at him like she hadn't even considered the scenario. And maybe she hadn't. Tough girls were forged in fire, not happy, easy lives.

He hoped somewhere far from the Bennett clan, Lilah spewed her own fire and snappy comebacks.

"I'm not sorry for putting myself between you and him, or trying to get him to leave town. That clan is poison, Sloan. They won't think twice about hurting a human. They'd probably welcome it." Truth speaker, he said to himself. He knew exactly how much they'd enjoy it. "We do things differently. That's what I'm sorry for—"

"You're sorry because we are different?" she interrupted.

"Yes. No. Not like that." He scowled. "I'm sorry because I didn't put stock in your way. I'm sorry I—"

"Utterly and totally dismissed my career?" Sloan rubbed a thumb over her fingernails, watching him from under her eyelashes.

The hint of mischief in her scent gave him pause. Lorne turned from her, but still watched her from the corner of his eye. "You're enjoying this."

"Always did love a good grovel."

She might be human, but she was as tough as any shifter he'd met.

He jerked his chin to the rowdy table in the corner. As he watched, Tansey blew a straw wrapped at Joss. Hunter fished out an ice cube from Joss's glass of water and aimed for Tansey, but hit Jesse instead. Ethan turned to growl an order and received a fry to the eye from his own mate, who widened her eyes with a look of innocence that could only mean intense guilt and zero remorse.

Disaster. They really shouldn't be allowed in public.

"I'd probably be out of a job," Sloan teased.

Lorne jerked. He lived in his head so much that he hadn't even realized saying the words aloud. Warmth spread through his chest at the approval in her eyes, though. "You want to join us? Can't guarantee they'll behave themselves."

She eyed the bag waiting for her, then the table of misfits. The hint of wariness entered her scent again, souring the sweetness of the fruit and cream.

Lorne held his breath. They were his people. If she would have anything to do with him, they were part of the deal.

She canted her head to the side and met his eyes. "I'd like that. Misbehavior and all."

## CHAPTER 13

Sloan leaned against the wall of the bar with a satisfied sigh. After polishing off enough barbecue to feed a small army, the Black Claw clan made their way across the street for after-dinner entertainment. They flipped a coin for darts or pool and then jostled to be the first to lay hands on a pool cue.

"You'll never make the shot," Alex griped as Lorne slowly strode around the pool table. The man grunted in answer and continued his serious study of ball placements.

"Ten bucks and a week of zero complaints about the breakfast menu says he can," Tansey challenged from her perch against the wall.

Alex slapped a hand over his heart. "I'm wounded that you would take his side over mine."

"I side with those who don't growl when they miss out on the bacon." Tansey swept her hair over her shoulder and leaned forward. "Joss tells me you're coming to the next movie and mani night."

Sloan wiped her smile off her face. Joss had been the one to approach her, but she put good money on the idea being sanctioned by the alpha's mate. "I said I'd think about it."

"Well, time's up. We're getting together next Monday. We have a lull in overnight guests and Joss owes me a hand massage."

"I do not!" Joss hiccupped next to her. Green eyes brightened unnaturally. "You're trying to take advantage of my weakened state."

"Damn right I am." Tansey laid her head against Joss's shoulder. "Will you please be amazing and pamper me? I'll pamper you back."

"Only if you're extra sweet to me and don't try to fight Hunter next time he tracks mud into the kitchen."

"There's a mat right outside the door. With a helpful reminder to wipe your damn paws. Alas, my hands will be gnarled monstrosities."

Joss chuckled and jerked her shoulder to throw Tansey off balance.

The micro-interactions were another reminder of where Sloan stood. Alone.

No lasting friendships. No one to go home to at night. The clan bickered and pushed each other's buttons like they were made for squabbling, but there was always a grin and a laugh to go with the jabs. They tried to include her, but she was still an outsider. She didn't know their inside jokes or when someone was pushed too far.

Outsider. That was her lot in life.

And then there was Lorne himself.

His eyes caught hers as he took his shot. That he wanted to watch her instead of the game he played woke something in her. She'd been watched by men before, of course, enticed and seduced by them, but none filled her with desire at the end of a single glance. Her skin tingled with warmth as if he'd passed a hand over her instead of just his gaze.

The connection broke when Ethan stepped between her and the pool table. Sloan swallowed hard. The loaded look still had her firmly by the back of the neck.

Ethan handed out the drinks in his arms while Hunter passed others to the men around the table.

"One girly beer for Joss, one stout for Tansey, and a water for the human."

Sloan raised her glass in a salute. She'd had a couple drinks at the barbecue joint, but she wanted to keep her wits about her. The shifters had metabolism on their side. "Thank you."

Lorne made his way to her side. He took a big swallow of the drink he'd told her to guard, then leaned closer. "They bothering you?"

She could almost feel his breath rustling her hair. Regardless, goose bumps lifted up and down her arms with a sudden awareness of him. Every single cell in her body seemed to sit up and pay attention to the man.

"They're harmless," she said. She tucked her hair behind her ears to give her something to do besides choke on the overwhelming sense of Lorne standing so close.

"Here's a question I've had and hasn't been answered. You talk about fated mates like it's some otherworldly, amazing thing. Is it just another word for a couple?" She'd tried to keep her voice low, but the improved hearing around her caught the words anyways.

Ethan and Tansey and Hunter and Joss turned to look at each other. Sparks danced in their eyes.

Sloan wasn't convinced they weren't laughing at her.

Alex, though, definitely snorted. Jesse outright grinned.

"This is the best the feds can do?" Lorne teased.

Sloan pointed at herself. Let them laugh. She was trying, dammit! "Human, remember? I wasn't exactly raised on this stuff. They gave us terms and definitions but in my experience, fate is just a fancy word for coincidence."

Tansey held out her arm. Two circles covered over each other to make a nasty scar. "Previously human, also not raised on this stuff." She traced the more jagged and shinier of the two. "Bitten by the animal form changes you."

"I know that much." They were trained to avoid letting a shifter, well, *shift*. Silver bullets and tranquilizers were standard issue, right along with silver handcuffs. Strong men and women were less of a danger than a rampaging beast that could put a human out of commission while she fought to control her new inner animal.

Ethan brushed his fingers over the other scar. Tansey fluttered her eyes shut and a pleased groan passed her lips. "Bitten in human form bonds you as mates."

Joss shook her head. "It's more than just some words. There's this whole other person outside of yourself, that matters more than anyone in the entire world. That you'd do anything for. It's like the world is one way, then suddenly it's different."

"And your animal knows. Just sits up and says that's the one, that's who I want for the rest of my life," Hunter added, lopsided grin growing as he stared at Joss. "There's no one way for it to happen. Growing up and slowly realizing—"

"Or having a gun drawn on you and being impressed at the sheer stupidity," Ethan interjected. Tansey flashed golden eyes at him, but her frown disappeared the moment he pressed his lips to her bite mark.

"Get a room," Alex muttered darkly. He leaned over the pool table and lined up his shot. The quick pull and release of the stick sent balls flying and crashing into each other, but none rolled into pockets.

"You deserved that." Ethan chuckled when Alex focused a glare at him.

"A mate is something many hope to find and most never do," Lorne added quietly. "Settling down happens, but it's not the lightning strike of fate."

Many hope. Sloan suddenly wanted to know if he

was among that number. "That still just sounds like words to me. So you're saying no one ever cheats or fights or runs off on their mate?"

"Well, no—"

"So then there's no difference. It's exactly like any other couple in the world. Good can happen the same as bad."

"That's just life. Mates are more," he insisted. His voice lowered to a rough rumble. "They're... important."

Important.

The word resonated, with him being at the very center of the waves vibrating through her. She couldn't put the feeling into any logical category. It didn't make any sense. Maybe to them, but Tansey had been human before and a couple of the guys in her unit had human mates. She couldn't explain why, when she shut her eyes, Lorne loomed large behind her lids.

"Cheat!" Jesse growled. "Alex is a cheat!"

Spell broken, the group turned to the tussle breaking out at the other end of the pool table. Jesse slammed a ball back to the surface and wrapped an arm around Alex's neck. The dark-haired men threw blows into one another, but even Sloan could tell they were pulled punches.

"Not a cheater!" Alex shouted with a wild laugh. "An opportunist!"

"Same thing!" Jesse spat back, adding another jab to the ribs.

"Your legal ruling, Agent?" Lorne asked.

Sloan wiped the grin from her face and jerked her thumb toward the ground. "Cheater! Punishable by the next round of drinks."

Whoops and cheers drowned out whatever snarky response Alex had for her. His eyebrows drew down in disapproval, but his eyes were as light as she'd seen them all night.

Lorne's slow smile made her feel like she belonged.

THE GROUP SPILLED out into the parking lot. Happy couples found their way to trucks with barely a wave over their shoulders. Single men, too, made quick departures, roaring engines to life and whipping out of their spots like it was a competition to see who could put wheels on the road first. Maybe it was. Everything turned to a game with the wild clan.

Alone, with only the sound of songs and a distant buzz of laughter from inside the bar, Sloan turned. Lorne leaned close enough that she could smell the drink on his breath. That, and more. Leather and cologne, maybe. The delectable notes twined together and made her crave another taste. Her throat tightened, and she sucked down a soft breath.

A little closer. Just a step. Her tongue swept over her lower lip in anticipation of another shattering kiss.

Lorne's lips hitched up into a smile and he brushed a bit of hair over her ear. Sloan's heart kicked against her ribs. The touch wasn't the one she wanted, but it spoke of a growing intimacy between them that went beyond straight desire.

"Come on," he said. "I have something to show you."

Sloan bit down on her tongue before she could pop off the name of random body parts.

Lorne held open the door of his truck and she brushed away his hands before he could help her inside. She could take care of herself, even if she liked a little bit of chivalry.

Three country songs later, Lorne pulled off the main road. Posted signs pointed arrows ahead for parking, trails, and a waterfall. "Where are we going?"

"You'll see," he answered. His hand fell on her thigh for the last bumpy stretch of road.

The parking lot was utterly deserted when Lorne pulled to a stop. Sloan pushed open her door and dropped to the ground before Lorne jogged around the hood. A frown crossed his features for a split second, then he turned on his heel and strode for the trees.

"This way," he called over his shoulder.

Sloan hesitated before hurrying to catch up. "How far are we walking?"

"Why, afraid of a little hike?"

She glared at his back. "No. I just can't see like you can."

He immediately turned back around and stooped. "Hop up."

"I can walk," she protested. "I just need a little guidance."

"Fine." Lorne offered her his arm. "Let me guide you like a little old lady."

She bit off her laugh. Old lady. Pfft. Just human.

She still linked their arms together. He waited until she took the first step and matched his stride to hers.

Warmth ignited under her palm. She stayed quiet and sank into the feeling.

Happy. For the first time in a long while, she felt happy. The stress of all the boggy, hard steps leading her to that moment, that walk through the woods, burned away under the slow roast of Lorne's touch.

A dull roar penetrated the fog Lorne poured into her head. The sound grew louder as the night pressed in around them and hints of civilization faded. She wasn't sure how far they'd walked when the path opened up on a small clearing. Off to one side, a waterfall poured over a ledge high above them. A narrow bridge passed across the middle for a picturesque scene. Like the river walk in town, a handful of benches waited alongside the banks for anyone wanting to take a moment to enjoy the scenery.

Lorne passed those by and walked down near the edge of the water. He'd left his hat on the dash of the truck, but the moonlight and trees above them shadowed his face. "Come here, Sloan," he said in a low voice. "Sit with me."

Her legs moved of their own volition. Not that she had anywhere else to be. The power he had over her was at once frightening and something she couldn't turn away from. Wouldn't. She played with fire the closer she got to Lorne Bennett, but she liked the burn.

Sloan took a seat next to him and drew her legs against her chest. For several long moments, they just sat. The quiet of the night sounded odd after the raucous night at the bar.

"This is where I come when I want to get some peace or when my bear gets riled up."

"Is he riled up now?"

Lorne blinked slowly. "Yes."

Oh, she liked that. It struck something primal inside her. Being the undoing of his control? That simmered her blood.

"Why did you invite me to eat with you tonight?"

Sloan held her breath and waited. She'd touched on a feeling of acceptance and belonging the night they'd visited the Summertime Fest together, but that ended with bruised egos and avoidance. She didn't want a repeat performance.

"I—" Lorne shut his mouth and shook his head like he needed to clear his thoughts. "I owed you an apology, and I wanted to do something nice for you. You wanted to figure us out. Now you know a little more about us."

"You didn't need to do that."

"No, but I wanted." He turned his eyes on her, barely moving the rest of his body. "How did you get here? Only human in that office. That has to be an interesting story."

Sloan frowned. That wasn't the direction she expected him to go. "I told you before. Not so interesting."

"No, you gave some abstract idea to avoid answering. Justice is not the steps taken."

The word wasn't exactly wrong, but he was right that she'd used it to keep her answer vague.

She stretched her legs out in front of her and leaned back on her hands. The stars were so bright between the leaves and branches above her. They weren't hidden away like they'd been back home.

Much like the shifters of Bearden.

"I jumped at the chance to join the Agency. I wanted to make a difference. I really do believe in justice for everyone. But that wasn't what I found." Sloan peeked at the man next to her and found him staring straight ahead. She turned her gaze back to the stars.

"Dirty cops. Hunters, I guess. At least some of them wanted to do lasting damage to any suspect brought through the doors. Most were smart enough to handle their business outside the building and keep it off camera. There wasn't much oversight or investigation into any claims of excessive force."

Important. Telling him everything felt important.

"My partner Jimmy was a piece of work. And I'm not talking normal police with a chip on his shoulder from witnessing so much shit. This man... well, he wasn't there with fairness or respect of the law in mind."

Lorne nodded, his mouth tightening.

Sloan picked at a stray string on her jeans. The words were as difficult as the first time she told them. She'd repeated them multiple times, written them down in report after report, and they still didn't flow off her tongue. "He bagged a suspect and instead of bringing him in, took him to an abandoned warehouse and tortured him. I made sure the bosses couldn't sweep it under the rug. Culpepper got a few years, and I got transferred here. I guess in their minds if I loved you lot so much, I should work with you."

"Punishment," he said flatly.

"Yep. Anything to get the Snitch Bitch gone." She bared her teeth at the night and her memories and all the assholes that tried to keep her in line. "Fuck 'em. I'm going to do my job."

"Tough Sloan," Lorne murmured. He reached out and ran down his hand down her back. The fiery anger that pulsed at the injustice of it all subsided as if he'd thrown her right into the middle of the water.

Sloan kicked her way back to the surface and reality. Maybe she'd had more to drink than she thought. The man had touched her. One touch, and her world felt…

One way, then another. Hadn't that been what Joss and Tansey said?

His fingers made another pass up and down her back. Sloan rolled her shoulders and sank into the relaxed feeling he induced.

"What about you? What steps brought you to Bearden?"

"A little bit of justice, and a whole mess of self-preservation," he deadpanned.

Sloan barked a laugh before shaking a finger at him. "Oh, no. That's my shtick. Get your own mysterious backstory."

"Not so mysterious. Not so respectable, either." He heaved a harsh breath. In the next second, he leaned forward and grabbed up a stick. The first snap of a twig sounded loud even over the rush of the waterfall. A leaf fluttered to the ground next. Lorne's jaw worked silently.

"You know what happens to shifters in the military? How they get booted to a furry squad?"

She nodded. "Crewe, our SAC, used to head up a unit. Some of the others served under him."

"Maybe it's better now, but the men who used to come back would have been better served if they were put down at the end of their tours. My father and all his brothers weren't good men when they came home. They wanted to hurt the ones that hurt them. Said we needed to watch ourselves and not let humans make another demand from us again. Military training, hatred of the government." He shrugged. "That was what I was born into and grew up around."

"Lorne, that's awful."

"I wasn't supposed to go near humans. I was supposed to be strong like my old man and uncles and cousins. I was supposed to prepare for a war that wouldn't ever happen.

"Instead, I liked a girl. And when my brothers and cousins—Ian included—found out, they decided to break us apart and teach us both a lesson. I don't even want to know what they would have done to Lilah if I hadn't found them. They tried to make me choose, make me kill her. I refused. I just wanted her safe. My brother Frank," Lorne's throat bobbed with a hard swallow. "Frank wouldn't let her go. So I fought him. Killed him. The rest of the clan would have killed me for it, for choosing a human over my clan, but I escaped before they could finish the job."

Sloan rolled her head to watch him. Her heart tore itself to pieces. She wanted to reach back in time and wrap arms around Lorne and his young love and keep them both safe.

Gold eyes locked on her again. "That's the difference between us, Sloan. Your justice isn't always compatible with mine."

"You're wrong. I see someone who stood up for someone else. I see someone who acted in self-defense."

"I used to be okay staying distant from everyone. Hard to make a place for yourself when you might need to run with just the clothes on your back. I even accepted they'd find me and put an end to the waiting. Started hoping for it." He rubbed at his chest. "Then Ethan found Tansey, and Hunter found Joss. I can't let anything happen to them. It'd be better if I left. But I want what they have. My bear wants it, too."

Her. He wanted her. The unspoken desire was written all over his face and in the eyes he turned on her. Gold churned in the depths, more that bright, shining color than his regular brown. She liked the balance he walked.

She wanted to see him slip, too.

They were more alike than she thought. He'd been set adrift at a young age. Her loss didn't compare to his, but the fraction she felt was enough to harden her against everyone else. She could only imagine what he'd been through to make such a man. They'd both been at odds with the people in their lives and uncomfortable in their own skins.

The world was one way, then another. That sounded about right. There was before-Lorne, and after. Before his kiss, and after.

She could keep falling back on old attitudes and throw up walls to keep herself from hurting at being the outsider, or she could turn into the force blowing through her life and maybe, for a second, let down her guard.

Stupid. Alone in the woods with a shifter that could just as easily eat her as anything else. But no, she trusted him.

And liked the hint of danger.

His nostrils flared and a delicious, cocky grin lifted his lips. "Agent Kent, do you have any idea what you do to me?"

Gone was her name, but the words didn't feel like he built a wall between them. They were flooded with a familiarity that pounded her heart against her breastbone.

"I thought we'd moved past calling me that."

In a flash, he had her on her back, wrists bound in his hands and stretched above her head. His head dipped, and he ran his nose down the column of her neck. "Calling you what?"

"Agent." She leaned up into his hold and nipped his lower lip.

His eyes rolled closed with a sexy groan. "Do you want me to touch you... Sloan?"

Her mouth dried at the smooth words. Sexy, tempting cowboy. Quiet and complex. Broody. His breath against her skin sent a shiver down her spine and she was glad she'd stopped drinking early in the night. She wanted to remember everything without a hint of fog.

Her throat worked. "Yes."

## CHAPTER 14

Lorne dragged his hand away from her captured wrists and cupped her neck. He stroked his thumb over her cheek, unable to help himself from rubbing against her silky smooth skin. His bear roared in the back of his head, claiming a victory Lorne wasn't willing to just yet.

She didn't believe in mates and fate? He wanted to prove her wrong.

He wanted to keep her safe.

He wanted to push her away.

She would drive him insane, Lorne vaguely thought. Her sweet taste, the whimpers that worked out of her throat as he deepened the kiss, the roll of her hips against his own. They were all binding him to her and her to him.

His bear had roared at him to care from the moment her scent tickled his nose. He'd dug in his heels and denied it all—and for what? A few more hours before arriving at this same conclusion? He couldn't keep away from her even when he should.

"You should run," he told her in a gravelly voice. "I'm no good for you."

"Feel plenty good right now," she breathed back.

He slid his hands under the hem of her shirt and caressed her silky skin higher and higher. He eased down the cups of her bra and lowered his head to the nipples poking sharply against her shirt. She arched into him as soon as he grazed his teeth over one stiff peak.

"Yes," she moaned softly. Her breath punched out from between her lips, hollowing her stomach. "Lorne, yes."

His bear chuffed with pleasure. Lorne echoed the emotion. Of anyone in the world, she was there with him. He had the chance to undress her and ran his hands over the curves she kept hidden under her clothes. Those were his, now. The swell of her breasts. Her round hips and thighs. All his.

His fingers worked at her jeans, popping the button and dragging the zipper down. More of her sweet scent hit his nose. Strawberries and cream and thick, delicious arousal. He wanted it all.

A deep rumble vibrated in his chest. "Fuck, sweetheart." He slid his hand down the front of her jeans and into the black lace he'd laid bare. Fuck, she was wet. Hot. His mouth watered for a taste of her. His bear roared to mark her.

*Mate.*

*Yes.*

*No.*

He settled on a 'not yet' and bringing her to release again and again until the light of dawn sent them about their lives.

He curled his fingers into her and loved the way her back bowed almost as much as he loved her inner muscles gripping him tightly.

Sloan dug her hands into his hair and claimed his mouth hard. He let off a low, rattling growl as her tongue clashed with his, twisting and tangling for more than a taste. She was losing control, losing herself in his touch, and he couldn't get enough.

She twitched under him as he delved into her with fingers and tongue. She writhed against his touch, kissed him harder, bit at his lip. Her thighs trembled and tightened with the helpless moan in her throat.

Close. By the Broken, what a glorious sight she was.

Lorne reared back on one hand and memorized the hungry look in her eyes and the red that colored her cheeks. Blonde hair, tangled and messy, framed her head like a damn halo. He doubted she'd take kindly to being called an angel, but that was what she was to him. A perfect, holy being he wanted to worship with his body.

"Want to watch your face when you come for me," he growled.

Red worked across her cheeks, but she didn't drop her eyes. His cock throbbed with that little act of defiance and confidence mixed into one.

Pleasure crested and her teeth caught her lower lip. Her shoulders pressed back against the earth and arched her into him for the final, resonating touches that squeezed her tight around him.

"Lorne," she moaned, choking back her cry.

*Mine.*

He'd fight everything to keep her. Ian, the rest of the Bennett family. Anyone who tried to stand between them. She belonged to him. He had to make her believe.

His objections buzzed and finally muted. The

world spun and recentered itself around the woman spread out under him and breathing hard.

Sloan flattened her hand against his stomach and slid down the front of his jeans. He sucked in a harsh breath the moment her fingers wrapped around his shaft.

"Careful, sweetheart," he murmured in her ear. "You start that and I can't guarantee I'll be able to stop."

Her breath hitched in the back of her throat. He could see the wheels turning in her head, weighing her options and the risks. He knew where he put his answer. Anything to sink into her.

She let go of a soft breath. "Someone could see."

Her scent thickened with the words. Fuck. The thought of getting her all riled up and feeling naughty had him almost harder than he could bear. He wanted to see her lose all her inhibitions completely.

"I bet you'd like that, wouldn't you?" He rolled his hips against her again and groaned as her fingers tightened around his cock.

"Lorne," she huffed a laugh.

"You started it," he baited. Gentleman that he was, he pushed to his hands. Rogue that he was, he pressed down and captured her lips for another quick kiss.

Finally on his feet, he offered her a hand up.

She darted away from him as soon as she had her footing. Eyes crinkling with laughter, she called over her shoulder. "I know where we can go."

Sweet fuck. He growled and stuffed himself back into his jeans. Merciful skies above, she would be the death of him.

He ran after her, bear pushing to the surface with concern. She'd needed help on the walk in, but every ounce of hesitation dropped away as she jogged ahead.

A growl rattled in his throat as his bear's worry turned to determination. Their mate wanted to play. He wanted to catch her.

His longer strides made quick work of her shorter ones. Another laugh bubbled out of her, grin stretching from ear to ear when she glanced over her shoulder. She darted to the side as soon as he got close, zigging and zagging to keep just out of his reach.

Tough girl. Tempting girl. She riled up his bear the longer she avoided him. Little human wasn't the one in charge.

He wrapped his fingers around her wrist and

jerked her to a halt. Spinning her around, he backed her up hard against a tree trunk, arms lifted above her head. Her panted breath sounded loud in his ears.

He rolled his hips against hers and grinned at the tiny noise that left her chest. "Didn't anyone warn you not to run from the beasts?"

She lifted her chin and met his eyes. "Maybe I wanted to get caught."

Growl on the tip of his tongue, he claimed her mouth in a harsh kiss.

RECKLESS. This was reckless.

It wasn't like she'd suddenly grown an exhibitionist side. No, it was all Lorne. Her blood bubbled in her veins with an utter need to feel him.

Leaning hard into her, he trailed biting kisses down her neck. A needy moan breathed past her lips as evidence of what he did to her. Those kisses, and the thick erection that hit her just right, were enough to want to strip down right there even if a thousand eyes watched from the bushes.

Sloan giggled and Lorne jerked his attention to her with a question written in his frown.

"Nothing," she whispered. "Just thinking what a bad influence you are. Turning me into a delinquent."

He blinked slowly, eyes brightening under heavy lids. "We're just getting started, sweetheart."

Her heart jumped in her chest. Dirty promise from a sexy man. She didn't need shifter senses to know he told the truth.

Sloan ducked under his arm and ran back down the trail and toward the parking lot. Home. They needed to get home before she combusted with need.

Lorne bit off his growl and raced after her.

Laughter spilled out of her lips as she ran. Reckless. Free. Her heart pounded with more than just the activity. He was dusting off cobwebs and setting up shop inside her chest and she wasn't flinching.

Then there was no sound except for her breathing. No footsteps followed her. No growls or laughs or puffs of air.

She slowed, then spun around in a circle. The spot between her shoulder blades prickled with the sense of being watched.

A branch broke, and she whirled to find nothing. Not even a darker, Lorne-shaped shadow.

Again, to her other side. Another snap. Closer. Her heart thudded against her chest.

*Don't run from the beasts.*

Yeah, she felt hunted. Her stomach dropped with excitement.

Lorne zipped from behind a tree and knelt mid-stride, throwing her over his shoulder. His hand came down on her ass with a hard smack that stopped her struggle. She was entirely in his thrall when that hand dipped between her legs and massaged her as he speed-walked to the parking lot.

Lorne threw open the door of his truck and let her fall on the seat. Gold eyes watched her as he followed her inside and pressed her back against the leather.

"I told you not to run," he said thickly.

Her thighs tightened involuntarily at the sound. Gritty and gravelly, all sexed up and animalistic. No one else could compare.

"I told you I wanted to get caught."

He toyed with her, that was abundantly clear. The strong hands holding her steady, the ease with which he flipped her over his shoulder. Lorne had control.

It wasn't something she usually enjoyed. Control was what she clung to when life threw curveballs at her. She couldn't stop those, but she could manage how she took them.

In his arms, she wanted to let go. She liked how he made her feel. Smaller, but no less important. He was stronger, but that didn't make her weak.

Sloan nipped at his earlobe and he groaned. He had control, but she wasn't powerless.

His fingers curled into the waist of her jeans. Gold eyes stayed on hers until she gave the tiniest nod. Then they swept down her body to the inches of skin he revealed.

"Fuck, sweetheart," Lorne groaned. His lids dropped closed and his nostrils flared like he needed to suck down her scent.

No one had ever looked at her like Lorne. His eyes held everything she wanted. Lust, desire, pure need. He wasn't scared of her or afraid to hurt her. They were just them, two people who were coming together for something fun.

No, not just fun. She couldn't put a name to it, wouldn't until she could be sure, but there was a tilting of the world around them.

Lorne pulled her jeans off her legs and knelt just as he tugged her to the very edge of the seat.

His tongue swept between her folds as expertly as his fingers earlier. Sloan pressed her fist to her mouth to keep her cry quiet. He licked and lapped at her like he couldn't get enough, satisfied groans filling her ears. His growl vibrated through her, too, buzzing against her like a damn toy and with twice the reaction.

Lorne drove his fingers into her and she was done. Her eyes clenched closed as pleasure ripped through her, nerves sparking all the way up her spine until she thought her head would burst.

She guided him up, heart pounding with every exaggerated movement. Hand next to her hips. Knee between her thighs. Elbow by her ear. He crawled up her body and settled between her thighs.

"Should make you beg," he said in his deep, gritty voice.

A shudder ran through her. Yes, begging. Yes, more. Yes to everything.

She shoved at his jeans until they were down his thighs and his cock pressed between their bodies. Sweet fuck. She knew what she'd felt before, but wrapping her fingers around him underscored just how long and thick he was. He hissed and bucked his hips with her firm stroke.

He had control, but she reveled in her power.

With a twist of his hips, he jerked out of her grasp and lined himself up with her slick entrance.

Lorne pushed to his hands. His eyes found hers, bright and gold and beautiful, at least until her own fluttered shut.

He pushed slowly into her, stretching her wide as he parted her with controlled thrusts. Shallow, deeper, an inch at a time. Maddening. Blissful.

Sloan caught her lip between her teeth just as he slid the last inch home. His strangled groan sounded like heaven. All for her. All because of her.

And then he moved and the stars he'd created before were a distant memory to the fireworks bursting behind her eyelids.

"Fuck, Lorne," she ground out in his ear. "Don't stop."

His growl vibrated through her and the world narrowed down to nothing but the sound of flesh coming together, growls and groans, and the feel of the sexy shifter filling her completely.

Lorne bucked into her faster. Harder. She could barely hold on, let alone breathe. He had her doped up and craving the next hit.

Pressure built in her middle as his thrusts turned harder and more erratic.

"Sloan," he growled. "Come with me."

Holy hell. She was close already, but the words prodded her closer to the edge of red hot passion.

She teetered right on the cliff until he rose up enough to bring his hand between their bodies. One swipe of her clit, another, and she arched into his touch.

"Lorne," she gasped as he roared her name.

He tensed, hips jerking again as warmth flooded her. He laid a biting, sucking kiss on her neck and stroked into her, throbbing out his release and pulling her aftershocks along with him.

When he finally collapsed against her, Sloan had a small smile on her lips. Euphoric. There was that word again. No wonder the Jimmy Culpeppers of the world were worried. They couldn't compete.

Her small laugh jerked Lorne's full attention on her, eyes sweeping to her face, then her neck. Worry creased his face. "Didn't expect that when I ran," she said in explanation. Bringing up Jimmy just didn't seem right.

He leaned back down and huffed a laugh in her hair. "Couldn't be helped."

With a groan, he stepped back, and they fixed themselves in satisfied silence.

"Where to, Agent?" he asked when he took his place behind the wheel.

Sloan swallowed. That was her out if she wanted to take it. She didn't feel a lick of shame or awkwardness. No desire to peel off from an ended date. Hell, she wanted more. She wanted to wake up to him.

Sloan glanced at him from the side. Strong jaw, covered in a scratchy beard. She'd never kissed a man with a beard before. She liked the sensitive rawness it left behind. "I'm not that far."

He gave her a hooded blink. "If that's what you want."

She met his gaze without flinching and nodded. Leftover warmth and new heat spread through her at the thought of not giving up on the night for many more hours.

Devilish grin on his face, Lorne lifted two fingers in greeting to the patrol car turning down the road just as they pulled away. "How does it feel to be a delinquent, Agent?"

Sloan passed a hand down her face and laughed.

# CHAPTER 15

Sloan rested her head against the window and watched the night blur. The woman in the reflection couldn't keep a smile off her face.

Next to her, Lorne let off a pleased sigh. His hand hadn't left her thigh since he started up the truck and drove them away from the park.

She liked that he wasn't one of those roll over and fall asleep sort of men, or the type who rushed out the door as soon as he finished. She didn't need a full-on cuddle session, but some intimacy was nice. The silent, content drive back to her place and the subtle promise of the night continuing kicked her smile up and warmed her blood by another ten degrees.

Sloan struggled to identify the feeling that

coursed through her. Physical euphoria from intense, star-inducing orgasms, sure. But the sensation went even beyond that. She felt solid. More real and centered and present than ever before. Like roots had spouted under her feet and secured her to the town and, more importantly, to Lorne.

She stood at the edge of something important. The dark side of a doorway, right where the light spilled from indoors. She was mere steps away from the place she needed to be.

Her logical side snorted. The thoughts were a little too woo-woo for her tastes.

At her direction, Lorne turned off the main road and down a residential street. "Surprised you aren't at the inn," he said.

He drove past a cluster of homes before making another turn down her street. Only a couple of neighbors lived near. Trees in the front yard hid most of her driveway, and the back butted up against wilderness. After years in a noisy city, the quiet was a nice change.

"I stayed there just long enough for my landlord to see I was a real person. I didn't want there to be any excuse to make this assignment temporary."

He glanced at her for a quick second. "You really believe there's good to be done there, don't you?"

"I do." Sloan lolled her head to the side and studied his profile. "Everyone deserves justice. I'd rather fight from the inside than give up on that idea."

Lorne turned up her driveway. Set off from the road was the small, one bedroom cabin she'd been lucky to snag. She'd panicked about her sudden move until the listing popped up. The little cabin had given her hope.

The headlights glinted off the ground in strange ways and Sloan straightened in her seat.

"Stay here." The words whipped out of her mouth as she jumped from the truck even before he pulled to a full stop.

"Like hell I will," Lorne growled.

Sloan shot a withering look over her shoulder. The noise bit off into a curse when she didn't stop. Between the man upset in his truck and the possibility of someone still on the property, she put her focus on the latter. Lorne's disapproval could wait.

Years of practice pushed her into high alert. She cataloged everything over the sound of her racing heart. Cracked and broken windows on her Jeep. Front door kicked in with wood splintered from the force of the blow. A dent behind where it banged into the wall.

She seethed. They wanted her scared and their tactics hadn't worked. Stalker photos and snake skins weren't enough to satisfy them. They had to up the ante and fuck with her personal space.

Assholes.

"Fucking Jimmy," she muttered.

"Who?" Lorne asked from behind her.

Sloan tried to hide her surprise. Freaking shifters and their silent steps. She really was at a disadvantage sometimes.

"Jimmy Culpepper." She spat out his name like it was poison. "My former partner. This isn't the first time he's sent someone to fuck with me because he's looking for revenge. They've just never been this destructive."

"They've done shit like this before?" Agitation rolled off the man in harsh waves. He shook his head, but it did little to clear the air between them. "One, you're going to tell me all about that. They don't get to do anything to you again."

So simple. A single, declaratory sentence. Sloan wished it was that easy. She'd have chanted it the entire drive across country.

She brushed past the broken door, shoes crunching on glass. The inside of the house was just as trashed as the outside, but she didn't have time to worry about the items needing to be replaced. The inventory could come later, once she had a chance to clear the house and make sure no one lurked in the dark corners. The shaking of her hands could start then, and she could give in to the violated feeling that pressed at the edge of her mind.

Right then, she wanted to secure herself.

Cautious steps forward, pausing to listen. She made her way into her bedroom and the gun safe she kept there. She punched in the code and drew out her weapon and badge, securing both to her waist.

Bathroom, clear. Bedroom closet, empty.

Motherfuckers wouldn't drive her off easily. They could rip up her couch cushions and break every dish in the cabinets, but they only pissed her off and made her dig in her heels. She had no intention of ceding any ground to vindictive assholes. They'd already forced her from one home. They didn't get to do it a second time.

Sloan was ready to breathe fire when she reached the living room again.

Lorne stood in the middle, slowly turning and surveying the damage. His chest heaved with rapid breaths and his fists opened and closed at his sides. A long, low growl rattled in his chest. "This was my fault. I led him right to you."

She paused and flicked her eyes to Lorne. The words didn't make sense. "You didn't do anything. This was Jimmy's people."

The dark edge of his voice didn't fade. "This was Ian. His scent is all over the damn place. Not even an hour old."

She stopped with her hand on the knob of the coat closet. No wonder he wasn't tearing the place apart to make sure no one was hiding away. He could smell if they were alone.

Her brain stuttered over the rest. Ian wouldn't have made even the top ten of suspects who'd trash her place. "Why? I didn't do anything to him. He has no reason to come after me."

"He wants me to suffer." Lorne scrubbed a hand through his hair and paced away from her, another growl sawing out of his chest.

"Well, fuck that. He's going to be disappointed." Sloan punched in the number to the office.

Lorne whipped back around. "What are you doing?"

"I'm calling this in." She gestured to the mess with her cell.

"I'll handle this." He reached over his head and pulled off his shirt. Darkened fingertips were a clear sign of his intention to go after Ian.

Sloan placed herself between him and the door, call temporarily forgotten. "You will not. That's not how the law works, Lorne. This isn't your problem."

"He came after you because of me. That's exactly how the law works." His fists tightened at his sides and his eyes flared gold. "I won't let him hurt you. Not like—He'll pay for this."

Not like Lilah. That was what he cut off.

Danger filled the air and coiled down her spine. Right alongside it was a feeling of...

No. She shoved away the sensation of belonging or being more than just herself. Those were idiot ideas when the man in front of her looked ready to commit murder.

"You've done your job. You figured out who did it. Now let the professionals track him down," she said calmly.

His upper lip lifted in a snarl. "My job? My job should have me out there right now. My bear is ripping me apart to make sure he never comes near you again."

"Look, I get you're all hopped up on some need to protect me. Back off. I can take care of myself."

He turned himself away from her and stared out the open door. "Not against this, you can't."

She bristled at the words. "Excuse me?"

How many times had she been told those words? How many people thought less of her for being a woman, or just plain human? She'd dried her eyes over the ones that nicked her heart and glared at the ones unworthy of anything else. Both groups lit a fire under her ass to prove them wrong.

To hear the words from Lorne, though, felt like a kick in the chest.

"You don't get to make some caveman claim over my safety," she spat.

"You're mine, Sloan. You have your way of doing things and I have mine." He took a step forward.

His? She didn't feel like it when he barely even looked at her. "Don't walk out that door, Lorne."

As pissed as she was at him doubting her, she recognized something in his voice that had been there when he told her his story. She'd heard the tone from others in his position of kill or be killed, save or let suffer. He'd torn himself apart for the decision he made so many years ago. He wouldn't fare any better a second time.

Damn the man for twisting her around into caring even when she wanted to slap him senseless.

"Or what, Agent? You going to shoot me?" His mouth twisted up in a savage smirk. "He's my problem, Sloan. He's only interested in you because of me. I won't let him hurt you."

She crossed her arms and stared at him coolly. "And if he was right here with his hand around my throat, I wouldn't fault you for getting involved. Going out there, tracking him down, that's the difference between defense and premeditation. I won't let you damn yourself."

A pause. He heard her, somewhere, but the part of him in the driver's seat didn't give a shit for her pretty words.

"Stay inside, Sloan," he said. The words were thicker than before. More inhuman. One shoulder jerked unnaturally. His other followed with a loud snap.

Lorne stepped through the door and swung his gaze back to her. Gold eyes brightened. "Stay inside," he said again.

His shape broke apart as she watched. Snaps of bone and tearing of muscle and skin made her stomach turn. She wanted to reach out and touch him, but he growled when she took a step forward.

Sloan closed the ruined door and pressed her back against it with a shuddering breath. When the sound of claws scratching against wood left her porch, she dared to peek through a broken window.

The dark bear stood taller than she imagined. He snuffed around her Jeep and his truck and lifted his head toward the tree line. Ten steps to one side of the house, then back to the other, the creature paced like a sentry on duty.

At least he wasn't off on some murder mission.

Sloan dialed the office and pressed her phone to her ear.

# CHAPTER 16

Lorne fit a wrench against a bolt and tried to ignore the shove of his inner beast. Repair work kept his hands busy, but his mind—and his bear—didn't take the hint and shut the fuck up.

The night still weighed down on him. It'd gone so well, then crashed into fiery ruin. Fucking Ian. Glass and ripped fabrics and broken wood were what he'd given Sloan on the night that should have been filled with slick skin and kisses.

His bear bristled and paced. The foul scent of his relative clogged his senses and erased all the good memories of Sloan.

Maybe he'd been saved from himself. The thought left a sour taste on his tongue. He'd come close to biting her. Claiming her. The mark from his kiss had faded by morning, but existed as a reminder of his lack of control.

That Sloan had been convinced to stay the night in his den was his only bit of solace. He hadn't even stepped inside with her. His bear wouldn't allow it. He'd shifted as soon as the door closed and kept a tight patrol around his home until dawn.

He'd brought Ian on Sloan. His fault. He should have kept away the moment he'd known Ian was in town. Any human he took a shine to was in danger from that very moment. But no. He just couldn't hold her at arm's length or forget she existed. She paid the price because of his weakness.

And what had he done? Shown his true colors. Let his anger get the better of him. His bear roared at him that they were protecting their mate, but Lorne knew better. He wanted to keep Sloan safe as much as he wanted Ian's blood. The two desires knotted together so thoroughly he didn't know where one began and the other ended.

He'd only held back tracking down the bastard because of her. Those big blue eyes pleaded with him not to chase after Ian. Her scent filled with concern for him. Selfless Sloan. She was too good to accept what needed to be done. Ian wouldn't stop until one of them was on a pyre to be burned.

She didn't want him to damn himself. Too fucking bad. He already lived in a hell of his own making. His conscience wasn't even a concern. He only wanted to keep her safe. He couldn't subject her to the harassment Lilah experienced.

He needed to stay away. He needed to keep her safe. He needed... fuck if he knew anymore.

His bear snapped at him. Lorne gritted his teeth against a fresh wave of sendings. Those happy moments his bear predicted weren't in the cards while Ian demanded his pound of flesh.

Round and round his thoughts spun, never coming to any solid conclusion. Stay. Go. Danger. Safe. He had no clear path forward.

He knew what he needed to do. A black hole filled his stomach whenever he came close to the thoughts. His bear slashed at his insides and promised to make life miserable.

Sloan would be better off without him.

He bared his teeth at the loose saddle rack and twisted hard at the stubborn bolt. The piece sheared clean off, and he punched forward into the plank jutting out from the wall.

"Motherfucker!" The metal crumbled around his fist. Lorne shook the sting off his hand and glared at the ruined piece of metal that should have been attached to the wall. Who needed a safe trailer, anyway? They should all just hide away and never leave the ranch again. Or make the damn tourists haul their own gear.

"How's it faring in here?" Ethan asked, poking his head through the doors.

Lorne turned his glower on his alpha. "Fine."

Ethan's eyebrows rose and his eyes lowered to the bent saddle rack dangling toward the floor. He didn't say anything, though, which made Lorne scowl even harder.

"Come on. It's about time to call it a day. You can fix that first thing tomorrow."

With a shrug, he pushed the ruined rack to the side. He expected Ethan to leave, but the man stood right by the open door and stared into the distance. Supposedly calm and relaxed, unease swirled in his scent.

"Had some trouble last night, I heard."

Lorne slid a glance to his alpha as he packed away his tools. He should have known. There was no avoiding the subject forever. He'd tried to keep it hidden, but word spread through Bearden fast when police and federal agents crawled over a scene. Silent questions had been shot his way all day. Ethan was the only one able to pin him down.

"You know we have your back in a fight if you need it."

"It's fine. I have it handled. No need to get involved." His fault. His problem. He hadn't wanted the clan to find out. They were likely to push in where they could get hurt. Ian was poison he wouldn't let harm the mates. He wouldn't let an ounce of his trouble rain down on the Black Claw clan.

"Lorne, I know what you do around here. You play aloof, but you're smoothing shit over with the Crowley pride or pushing buttons to get a brawl going before anyone can get it on tape."

Lorne grunted. Ethan would only smell the lie in his denial.

"That doesn't go unnoticed or unappreciated. I know it's not your way to ask for thanks or help. You have both."

"Don't need it," he said gruffly.

"Bullshit." Ethan cocked his head. "My unwelcome advice? Caring from the background isn't going to work with your mate."

Lorne snapped the toolbox closed and stepped out into the yard. "She's not my mate."

His bear ripped him to shreds.

*Deny, deny, until we die.*

Better this way. The brief moments of believing he could make a life with her were done and gone. He had to stiffen his spine and plant himself firmly against the trouble brewing in the distance. Sloan would be safer without him. He'd make sure of it.

He was bad for her. Damage had been done long ago. He wouldn't stain her with the blood on his hands.

Ethan barked a laugh. "I said the same thing once, too. Now, look at me."

"Tied down and browbeaten?"

"And steadier than I've ever felt." Ethan rubbed at his chest right over his heart. "Tansey means the world to me, just like I think this woman is to you."

Lorne stayed silent.

"Your people know who she is now. There's only one way to keep a woman like that safe."

"Pack up and put distance between us."

"No. Idiot," Ethan snorted. "She's determined to stick her foot in your trouble. All you can do is stay by her side and fight the fights she refuses to let go. Otherwise, who's going to be there when she pushes too far?"

That was... something he hadn't thought of. She was a fighter. Had to be, from what she'd told him and what he'd guessed about the rest. Clearing out the threat of Ian would keep her safe on one front. She'd find ten more battles by the end of the day, probably.

His bear rumbled in his head, as close to a purr as the beast could manage. Sticking close to the tough woman meant keeping her safe. He'd been an idiot to think otherwise, according to the sendings from his bear.

Lorne cocked his head at a noise in the distance. An engine rumbled closer and his bear answered with a pleased sound of his own. He glanced over his shoulder and saw the green Jeep bouncing along the dirt road.

"You want this woman?" Ethan asked quietly.

Sloan's pulled to a stop, and she dropped to the ground.

"Yes." The word punched out of Lorne. His chest ached with its utterance.

It'd been given life. There was no taking it back.

His life shifted the moment he scented Sloan. There was no going back to a world without her.

"Then you need to be upfront with what you want. Caring from the background won't work with mates. She'll call you on your shit more than we do. Rightfully, too." Ethan slapped him on the back. "Now's the time to figure out where you belong."

"I'm going to be terrible at this." Lorne raised a hand in greeting to the woman behind the brand new windshield. She ducked her eyes for a brief second, then met his look with a wide smile.

"Nah," Ethan countered. "You've had practice caring for the rest of us, and I'm sure you hated us sixty percent of the time. You'll be great when it's the person who makes you feel whole."

His alpha slapped his back once more, then started toward the main house with a tip of his Stetson for Sloan.

Sloan rounded the front of her Jeep. Strawberries and cream filled his nose and the words he'd prepared sat on the tip of his tongue, stunned into silence.

*Mate.*

The roaring and clawing of his inner animal ceased the moment he'd caught sight of her.

And now? His bear was in utter awe of her. She hadn't flinched when confronted by Ian's damage. Nor had she backed down when he was ready to give in to all that pent up rage.

Lorne wanted her. For another night, a month, an eternity. She was steel wrapped in silk. Good packaged in toughness. He could almost believe in her idea of the future. Nothing would stand in her way of achieving the justice she wanted for everyone.

She brushed back the stray locks of hair that had escaped her bun during the day and flashed him a cautious smile. "You had my Jeep fixed up."

"Least I could do." He'd arranged for the window repair as soon as she left that morning. His family, his problem. She didn't need to pay for the damage Ian inflicted.

"The rest of the mess should be cleaned up and fixed by tomorrow or the day after, according to my landlord." She hesitated. "I can get a room at the inn. Or up at the house. August and his family have a couch they've offered me, too. I don't want to put you out for another night."

"Stay. Here."

Sloan ducked her eyes for a brief second before bringing them right back to his face. "Do you mean that?"

She didn't hide from the uncomfortable parts of life.

He leaned close enough for their breath to mingle. "Yes."

Lorne cupped her cheeks and kissed her soft and slow. No rushing, simply letting her scent cascade over him was enough to send his bear spiraling into delirium. Him, too, if he was honest. And when she parted her lips and let him slip his tongue against hers, he was done.

He trailed his palms down her shoulders and arms, then squeezed her hips. He skimmed over the swell of her ass and hauled her into his arms.

"Lorne," Sloan laughed against his lips. "Put me down."

"Not happening." He didn't stop until he reached his door. "I missed you."

The words were heavy with extra emotion. Sloan lowered her lids and watched him from under her eyelashes. Strong jaw, troubled eyes. She didn't need to be a shifter to sense the conflict in him.

"Did you?" she asked softly "You didn't even stay with me last night."

"A mistake." Lorne fumbled open his door and kicked it closed behind him before backing her against it. "One I aim to fix. If you'll have me." He shook his head. "I don't know how to do this, Sloan."

"You're getting awfully good at apologizing." Her lips twitched before she turned serious again. "Let me in, Lorne. That's how this works. What happened last night?"

Big. Important. That feeling of the world shifting took hold all over again in the silence of his home.

Nothing had changed since she left that morning. The worn couch still sat against one wall. The drying rack had the same dishes in it. Even the curtain on the back door hung at the same angle where she'd twitched it aside to watch the prowling bear.

The feeling of change didn't leave her, though. She held her breath and waited for Lorne to say something.

He pressed his forehead to hers, eyes closed. When he opened them, they were pure gold. "I was scared," he choked out.

"You could say murderous, even," she murmured.

"The idea of anyone trying to go after you—"

A growl rumbled in his chest and kept going until she pressed her fingers right over his heart.

"You make my bear wild." He wrapped his fingers around hers and flattened her palm against his racing heart. "That's all for you, sweetheart. Last night... I needed to protect you. That was all my bear wanted in that moment."

"I needed you with me, not out chasing someone

down and causing more trouble. You can't protect me from everything. I know what I signed up for, Lorne. There's always someone out there wanting to hurt others. Sometimes that might touch my life."

She didn't cater to fragile egos. They'd been the death of more than one relationship. She didn't want to believe Lorne was cut from the same mold. At least he seemed stuck in wanting to protect her, instead of trying to play down her own ability.

"But when it's my family doing the hurting, I can't stand by. This isn't a little dispute that will blow over. Ian could be summoning the whole damn clan on our heads right now.

Sloan shook her head. "I don't think there's anything left of them."

Lorne quirked an eyebrow at her. "What do you mean?"

"I mean," Sloan paused and chewed on her lower lip. It wasn't really confidential information, or anything significant to an investigation. He could discover it for himself with a few phone calls, proba-bly. "I mean, the information we have says there are only a handful of Bennetts living where you grew up. Reasons unknown, but the theory is the clan split years ago. Ian seems to be on his own."

Confusion lined his features, then a flicker of sadness. Grief faded into relief.

Every one of the emotions she saw play out on his face had a place in his life. They were still his family, no matter what they'd done to him. He could mourn the loss of who they should have been and still be happy they wouldn't be a threat to him or anyone else.

"Good," he said finally.

She heard the lie in his voice. He put on a brave act, but the darkness visited upon him wouldn't go away so easily. Wounds like his took years to heal, if they ever did.

Sloan hoped he could let go enough of the past to live in the present.

He leaned into her palm when she pressed it to his cheek. A rumble vibrated through his chest, and through her, still wrapped up in his arms.

"I'll stay," she said, "but only if you're here with me. I need you in this, not guarding against something from the outside."

Gold eyes still sparkled at her, but the trouble in them transformed into a different kind of mischief. "I think you can make it worth my while."

Heat flared in her core, but she wasn't willing to

give in so easily. "Shouldn't you make it worth mine? I'm not the one that left the bed cold last night."

"Let me make you dinner." He rubbed at his chest. The growl in his throat deepened for a single note. "I can provide for you, even if I couldn't protect you."

"Down, bear. I can take care of myself."

"Easy, human. Instincts you don't understand are demanding I care for you." He let her slip to the ground, but he didn't back away.

"What are they like?" she asked without meeting his eyes.

The SEA had manuals on the different supernatural species. Vampires, fae, and shifters all had their own way of living, and subsets of those groups added complexity. With shifters, great attention was paid to instinctual responses. Providing, protecting, those were big between mates. She still had a hard time wrapping her head around the idea of it being *more* than a simple relationship, but she couldn't deny the reverence with which the word was spoken.

"I wanted to rip Ian apart last night. That's a big one," he answered after a long moment. "Mostly I wanted to get you away from there. He could have come back, and he didn't deserve to even put eyes on you after all the damage he did."

"And now?"

"I want…" he frowned, like he didn't know what words to use. "I don't want to see you lose your smile. I want you happy."

Sloan wrapped her arms around his neck. "Then you better get to cooking, cowboy. I didn't stop for lunch today."

Lorne chuckled and leaned into her again. He sipped at her lips. Peck, sip, he held himself back from turning those little kisses into more. They were building something inside her, though. Something powerful and needy. He was making it harder for her to turn her back on him.

She didn't have his powerful instincts, but she definitely wanted to care.

# CHAPTER 17

Sloan's eyes snapped open. Her pulse kicked up a notch, and she struggled to figure out what woke her.

Pressure on the bed shifted and feet dropped to the ground. "Stay here," Lorne whispered fiercely.

"What's going on?"

Instead of answering, he padded on silent feet to the window and flicked aside the curtain.

She couldn't see his face. Hell, she could barely see anything in the darkness. But she recognized the tight set to his shoulders and rigid spine. The man was on alert.

"Lorne, what is it?" she asked again.

A low growl rattled in his chest. "Don't worry about it. I'll take care of this."

The words chilled her. He'd said the same thing when her house had been vandalized and he wanted to tear after Ian. She'd had a devil of a time talking him down then. She doubted he'd listen a second time.

Lorne swept away from the window and past the bed. "Stay here," he ordered over his shoulder.

Sloan listened to him as long as she could. Twelve steps, maybe. She didn't even hear a door open or close.

She swung out of bed and pulled on jeans as she crossed to the window. Lorne's glance out left a tiny part between the curtains. Someone stooped near the tires of his truck. Good money that it was Ian.

"Motherfucker," she muttered. One home wasn't enough of a message for him. He had to keep picking, keep attacking. He couldn't let Lorne have any peace from the crimes and traumas of years past.

And Lorne? Sloan had no idea where he'd disappeared to after ordering her to stand down. She was a damn agent; she should be the one running around in the dark and chasing after suspects. She couldn't let him dive down a path that would lead him to ruin.

She stuffed her shirt over her head as she rounded the bed and reached for her phone to punch in Crewe's number. Two rings, and he picked up. "Better be good, Kent," he muttered.

"I have eyes on Ian Bennett. Possible property damage in progress." Sloan cradled the phone between her ear and shoulder while she tugged on her shoes.

All the sleep dropped from his voice. "Where are you?"

"Black Claw Ranch."

He paused. Either with disapproval or jotting it down, Sloan didn't know. "Got it. Stay put, you hear? Do not move until you have backup."

She made a noncommittal sound and hung up the phone.

Lorne and Crewe both could tear strips from her hide after Ian was brought to justice. She'd take the reprimands when she was sure Ian wouldn't kill Lorne. No doubt about it, her cowboy would end up dead either in the true sense of the word or as good as, if he were forced to repeat the actions of his past.

She tossed her phone to the bed and stepped out of the bedroom. No one stood in the living room. She strode for the back door and out into the night.

Sloan paused at the corner of the house and listened carefully with her back pressed to the wall. No sounds reached her ears. Not a breath or a step or anything else that would give someone away. Unease crept up her spine with the feeling of being hunted just as she'd had on the trail with Lorne. Only instead of a stomach-dipping night of pleasure ahead, a monster waited in the dark.

She kept low as she rounded the corner. No movement caught her eyes. Both men had vanished into the darkness.

Sloan slipped to the side of her Jeep and unlatched the door as quietly as possible. Metal still creaked. Grimace on her face, she unlocked and fished into her glove compartment for her weapon, badge, and handcuffs.

Now to find Ian.

She glanced behind her and toward Lorne's home. Others were arranged nearby with no lights on inside. The barn and main house loomed large in the other direction. Without any signs, she didn't know which way to go.

Something clattered to the ground in the distance. Sloan swung her weapon in the direction of the barn. Adrenaline dumping into her veins, she started into the night.

Not a living thing moved or made a sound. No bugs, no critters, and certainly no humans or shifters.

She felt exposed.

Sloan hurried across the open expanse and toward the barn, hoping she wasn't about to find Lorne covered in Ian's blood. None of the side doors were thrown open, so she stuck close to the fence ringing the building. The double doors of the entrance were parted just enough to allow someone the squeeze inside.

Sloan raised her weapon. Two quick breaths, and she swung the nearest door open.

She passed her eyes over the scene quickly. Ian moved down the lines of stalls, peeking into each of them. Sloan's eyebrows drew together. Was he looking for a place to hide or a way out?

With a muffled growl, he stopped at one stall and yanked on the bolt holding the door closed.

"Stop where you are," Sloan called out. She trained her weapon on the center of his back. Going for a horse? Bastard.

"You're not the one I expected to come running." Ian shuffled slowly around to face her. A malicious grin hitched up his lips. "You fighting all that fuck-er's battles?"

"You're even dumber than you look if you think that's the case." She took a step to the side, weapon still trained on Ian. "On your knees. Let's not make this more of a problem than it already is."

Looking downright feral, Ian nodded. He slowly raised his hands and laced his fingers behind his head, then dropped to his knees.

Unease rolled through her again. Sloan kicked the feeling to the back of her head. She didn't have any time for the doubts brought with it. Ian was her priority. The rest could be dealt with once he was in custody.

She holstered her gun at the same moment she whipped out the handcuffs. With a flick of her wrist, the pieces snapped open and she settled the claws around the first of Ian's wrists.

He jerked just before she could ratchet it closed. Body twisting, he swung a fist into her stomach.

Sloan doubled over and wheezed. Her lungs refused to work and Ian gave her no time to recover before another brutal pounding cracked against her ribs. She stayed upright by sheer stubbornness and locked knees.

She stumbled backward and away from the source of pain, hands already reaching for her weapon. Stony determination covered over slick fear. She wouldn't go down without a fight.

Ian clicked his tongue in disappointment. "Now, now, you shouldn't point guns at people."

He yanked on the grip and ripped it away from her. She winced as the weapon clattered to the ground and skidded away from them both.

Fight or flight scratched at the back of her brain, two sides of the same instinct warring with the other. He was stronger and meaner. He had the advantage over her even without factoring in the beast under his skin.

Help was on the way. Maybe even somewhere in the night already. Others lived on the ranch, too. The wild clan would be down for a fight.

Sloan took a step back. She just had to buy herself some time.

*Don't run from the beasts.*

Lorne's words echoed in her head.

Fuck it. Sloan glared at the man and prepared for the next attack.

Another punch to her stomach, a knee to her already aching ribs. She lashed out between blows, landing a cracking punch to his nose. Her knuckles complained, but she gritted her teeth against the pain.

Blood spurted and anger shined in his eyes. Ian wiped at his lip with the back of his hand. "I'll give you this much, you got more spirit than that last human cunt."

"Yeah? Did she hit as soft as you?" she taunted. Her body protested the next step she took backward. Another made Ian shamble forward to reach her.

Ian snarled and lunged for her. Sloan danced out of his reach. Ten steps more, maybe less, and they'd be out in the night.

Sloan turned and ran. Six steps. Four.

She passed through the barn doors to the sound of whinnying horses.

Ian yanked her hair and dragged her to her knees.

Sloan twisted in his grasp and fell on her back. She lashed out with fists and kicks, but Ian brushed them off like they were flea bites. All the fear and anger she'd locked away rode up again the moment he straddled her and raised his fist.

Beaten. Weak. Stupid. Words flung at her over the years forced their way to the front of her mind.

A roar cracked through the night and a huge bear raced toward them.

Ian's eyes widened with loathing and a spark of fear before he scrambled to his feet and ran.

Pops and cracks echoed in her ears as the bear's shape shimmered. Lorne crouched over her, hand smoothing back her hair. Horror and guilt played out over his face as he made soothing noises. "Shh, shh, it'll be okay.

"Stop him!" Sloan gritted out.

Lorne didn't move. "I'm not leaving you like this."

He held her through all her protests while the rest of the clan stumbled out of their homes. He didn't let her go until lights flashed over them.

"I'M FINE," Sloan insisted, but the doctor still held her chin between strong fingers. Icicles, maybe. The gloves didn't offer much barrier between him and freezing her. She thought she'd die of exposure before the exam was finished.

The door to the exam room burst open. Crewe bustled inside, huge shoulders nearly hitting the edges of the doorframe. "Kent, what were you thinking?"

Lorne followed on his heels. "How is she, Doc?"

That question was no less demanding than the first, but was laced with more concern.

The old man clucked his tongue and finally released her chin. He reached for her chart and made a note before clicking his pen and stuffing it back into a pocket. "Black eye, but no threat of permanent damage. I'm concerned about the bruised ribs. No break that I could see, but those can be a nasty bit of work for recovery."

"Hi. Right here," Sloan bristled.

He blinked at her like he'd just realized she existed. "Right. Yes. You're in for some rough days, missy. You humans heal so slow."

Sloan cocked her head and tried to puzzle out if he was simply stating a fact or insulting her to her face. The man's bedside manner was astoundingly lacking. It was a relief when he scuttled from the room and left her alone with the stone-faced men bracketing her bed.

Crewe fixed her with a steady, no-nonsense look that probably made plenty of underlings squirm. She fought against the desire to duck her eyes.

"You need to rest. You take all the time you need. I don't want you back at the office until you're completely healed up."

The words grated. Time. Completely healed. They sounded nice on the surface, but she knew they drew a line between the shifters and the human. She *lacked* when compared to them.

Crewe could take his kind words and choke on them.

Sloan struggled upright and only hissed once at the sharp sting of pain from her bruised side. "I need to get back out there. Who is tracking him?"

"Not a chance, Kent. You're beat to shit. Let the rest of us handle this. You did what you could. It's time to back off. You're too close to this." Crewe lowered his eyes. Frustration greeted her when they opened again. "And that's not taking into account the orders you disobeyed when you didn't wait for backup."

"Of-fucking-course I'm close. He's fucked with me twice now. I couldn't let him get away."

Both Crewe and Lorne cocked their heads. Nostrils flared.

Well, it wasn't a complete lie. She wanted to catch Ian as much as she wanted to keep Lorne from doing something he'd regret.

"He's right. You need to rest. This isn't your fight," Lorne said.

Sloan slowly swiveled her attention from Crewe to Lorne. Her jaw tightened to hold back the string of curses she wanted to unleash on both of them.

Crewe cleared his throat. "I'll let you two have a moment." He patted the railing on the clinic bed, then pointed at her with a stern look. "You're off duty until you're healed up, understand?"

"Understood," she agreed unwillingly. The moment the door shut behind him, she started in on Lorne. "Did they find a trail? Are they searching for him now? Why the hell did you go out there by yourself?"

"I could say the same about you. It's not your fight," Lorne stubbornly repeated. His eyes trailed down her face as he studied her injuries. Regret brightened his eyes, but his voice was hard when he spoke. "Look at what he did to you."

Sloan glared. "This isn't the first time I've been slapped around by a suspect. Won't be the last. It's a part of the job, Lorne. A shitty part, but not unavoidable."

"It was! Entirely unavoidable!" He jammed his fingers into his hair and paced away from the side of the bed. On his turn back, his eyes flared gold. "If you had just stayed inside like I said—"

"So you could go out there and kill him yourself? You do not get to order me around like a child. I know the risks—"

"With *humans*. You aren't one of us. Going up against a shifter left you looking like this!" He waved a hand at her.

Sloan recoiled, then shook her head. "That's right. I'm not one of you. Let's just keep underscoring that point, shall we? I'm not one of you, so your psycho cousin wants to kill me. I'm not one of you, so I should just forget about upholding any laws that touch someone with supe blood. I'm not one of you, so I should probably invest in a fucking bubble and live out my life in perfect safety."

"That's not—"

"That's exactly what you meant. You and everyone else who takes a look at me and scoffs because I'm not as strong as you, or I don't heal as fast, or because I'm just another human. Nothing special, right?"

His eyes flared gold. "No," he ground out. "You're entirely special. I don't want to see you hurt like this ever again."

She heard the unspoken words that had soured the air between her and so many other relationships. None of this would happen if it weren't for her job. If she just gave it up, worked somewhere else, did anything else, she wouldn't land in a clinic with bruises and black eyes.

Fuck that. Anyone who doubted her didn't need to be in her life.

"You should leave." She sank back against the bed and turned her face from him.

Her heart ached and she couldn't even convince

herself it was because of Ian. That was the danger of letting someone in. And he'd let her down like all the rest.

"Sloan," he said in a strangled voice.

She didn't move. She didn't look at him. Lorne wasn't her concern. She hardened herself against the pain she'd been stupid enough to let him cause.

Finding the asshole who fucked him up was her entire focus. She could give Lorne that much before forgetting about him completely.

## CHAPTER 18

"Turn here," Sloan said. She pointed to the rundown strip mall with two good stores and a bar on one side. The drinking hole claimed the biggest slice of vehicles in the parking lot.

"This is not a doctor's office," August grouched.

"You're very perceptive."

"'Had an appointment,'" he muttered, shaking his head with disbelief. "You've been spending too much time with us."

"Maybe," she conceded. She'd been purposefully vague on what she needed when she asked for a ride. She needed her words to pass the sniff test so her partner didn't guess anything was amiss. His fault for assuming her appointment was with an actual doctor.

August eyed her sharply. "What the hell have you gotten me into, Kent?"

Well, there was always going to be a moment of confession. She couldn't very well track down Ian without someone's help. And she *would* track him down. Her stomach churned with the idea of him out in the world, making anyone else miserable. That, and she needed to prove everyone wrong about her.

A tiny, minuscule voice in the back of her head corrected her. Not everyone. Lorne.

She wasn't weak. She wasn't incapable. Being human just meant she had to work in other ways. And no way in hell was she going to see some criminal activity taking place and fall back asleep.

That tiny voice squeaked about making sure the asshole didn't get close to Lorne again. Or the other way around. Lorne didn't need that trouble.

She shoved that voice way down deep and drowned it out with answering August. "We're looking for Ian."

Lorne wasn't her concern. He made it known what he thought of her job and her ability to do it. The sting of his rejection mattered less than putting a collar on his cousin. Ian Bennett was dangerous and needed to be stopped before he did anyone else harm.

"Fucking hell!" August slapped the steering wheel then shoved a finger under her nose. "I knew you'd be the death of me."

Sloan went on as if he hadn't objected. "We know he was staying in Oxmark when we brought him in for questioning. We know he likes to have a drink. So I got a list of bars in the area. We'll start near his motel that he won't go back to unless he's the biggest idiot in the world because of course, that's the first place someone will look for him. Not us, though. Because we're not idiots."

"Okay, one, this is some bullshit. I resent being tricked into a stakeout on my day off. Two, how the fuck did you not account for someone else in our office doing the same shit? Crewe could roll up here any second and see your sorry, busted-looking ass and then rip into me for driving you out here."

Sloan looked over one shoulder, then another. She made a show of squinting in the distance with a hand over her eyes before giving August a flat stare. "Don't see anyone else here, do you?"

"And if he is here, what then? You going to roll up in a wheelchair and knock his legs out with a crutch?"

"I don't have either of those, so no." She shrugged a shoulder. "But I guess if you don't want any commendations for bravery or some other bullshit, I'll go find some."

"Motherfucker," August muttered with another shake of his head. "What's your mate think about this?"

She tracked a car pulling into the lot and parking near the bar. When a blond man exited the vehicle, she relaxed back against her seat. Not Ian. "My what?"

"Oh, come on. You've been drooling over him since those horse-riding hicks left dust all over the office."

"I don't know if they'd like being called hicks," she said lightly, hoping he'd take the hint. Discussing whatever complicated mess that tangled her up with Lorne wasn't on the books. Find Ian. Check out some bars. Forget Lorne existed. Those were her goals for the day.

August apparently didn't want to cooperate. "You're telling me he hasn't said a word? Damn, girl. You're both fucked up. I told Alicia the moment I got her name."

Sloan snorted. "That sounds romantic. 'Hi, I'm

August and I'm here to leave you unsatisfied for the rest of your life. Let's get some rings.'"

"Bite marks, and it took some convincing. For the record, she has never been left unsatisfied." He dropped his wrist over the steering wheel and studied another car rolling slowly through the lot. "She was human, like you. I had to work my ass off to convince her I wasn't crazy. Then I had to convince her I wasn't any danger once she saw my bear. Once all that was out of the way, then she was more understanding. But you know about this life already. You didn't have the surprise factor."

"So I'm just supposed to drop my panties and leave all objections at the door?" she snapped. "Don't I get a say in the matter?"

"You're not picking him back?" He shot her a dumbfounded look.

"I don't know what I'm doing, August. Knowing some of the process on paper doesn't really prepare you for the real thing."

Or the disappointment when it didn't work out.

Instinct picked the person, that was what the manual said. Well, she didn't have an animal inside doing the talking. All she had were past experiences and current behavior. She didn't take anyone's shit then, and she wasn't about to start now. She wouldn't be ordered to give up doing what she loved because someone decided she would be safer.

A man and a woman walked out of the bar and shambled toward an old brown pickup. He cracked open the door and held out a hand to help her inside before rushing around to take his place in the driver's seat.

Sloan rubbed a hand over her heart. Even the damn barflies had each other while she was alone.

"How do you feel right now?"

"Like I got hit by a train." Not a lie. Her ribs felt like they were on fire and the side of her face throbbed with every beat of her heart.

"Below all this." He waved a palm at her. "You feeling heart sick? Clenched up stomach? Chills and dry mouth and like you're in the worst hangover of your life?"

Reluctantly, she nodded.

"That's the bond. That's cutting ties to your mate. If you're feeling this bad, he's got it ten times worse being an actual shifter."

"I'm glad we can make this about him," she sniped.

August raised his hands in surrender.

Sloan chewed on her lower lip. There was no living without pain, but she hated to be the cause of it.

After a beat of silence, she asked, "Will it pass?"

"Probably for you. I didn't fight fate, so I can't tell you about that. All I can say is there's nothing Alicia and I can't overcome. She hates where I kick off my boots at night and wants to strangle me five days out of seven, but she's it for me, just like I am for her. That devotion runs bone deep. I wouldn't give it up for the world."

She envied the man and his certainty. The thought of someone at home, ready to be irritated at her, warmed her heart. Her mother had done the same for her father. Like August, Sloan never questioned the underlying affection.

She had no doubt that both couples supported their partners in every aspect of their lives. The warmth in her middle died to a cold breeze through the empty chambers. She couldn't count on that with Lorne.

Ian stepped out of the bar and saluted them, cutting her pity party short.

"Shit, you might just be good police," August snarked. "Get Crewe on the phone and backup this way."

She pulled her phone from her pocket and started dialing. Her gaze stayed trained on Ian as he paced from one end of the bar front to the other. He didn't turn back toward the door when he reached the corner.

No. No, no, no.

The phone kept ringing.

"Where is he going?" August leaned to the side to try keeping eyes on him.

"Back inside maybe?"

"Stay here, will you? I'm going to keep eyes on him."

She waved him on. "All yours."

Sloan watched through the windshield as August approached where Ian disappeared. Her breath caught in her throat as she imagined how the conversation would go. Asking Ian to come peacefully, saying they had some questions for him back at the office. Getting a little more forceful when Ian undoubtedly refused. She even wouldn't mind seeing him flattened on the ground and cuffed before being transported. Seemed appropriate for the bruises and stiffness she'd carry for the next few weeks.

Crewe finally answered right before the call went to voicemail. "What is it, Kent?" he growled.

"August and I have eyes on Ian Bennett."

He paused for a heavy second. "Please tell me you're joking."

An SUV with the SEA logo blazoned across the side roared into the parking lot. A second, then a third, followed.

What the hell?

Two of the vehicles slammed to a stop right near the bar entrance, but the last swerved around to block her view of the scene. Crewe jumped out and strode for her, and yanked open the door.

"Where's Snow?" he demanded. Sunglasses hid his eyes, but Sloan put good money on them being the bright color of his inner animal.

She blinked in confusion, then pointed toward the corner of the bar. "He followed Ian. We didn't want him slipping away before someone else got here."

"Shit," Crewe cursed. He gestured some of the others forward, then ducked back to her. "Do you have any idea the shitstorm you've brought down on my people? Ian Bennett called *us* to report fearing for his life."

She slammed a fist against the dash. "Motherfucker."

"That's not all." Crewe looked like he'd swallowed an entire storm and was ready to unleash it on the next person who pissed him off. "There's an Internal Affairs agent that wants to talk to you."

Fuck.

SLOAN LEANED against the wall of the room and glared at the door. At least her executioner waited in another box, ready to interrogate her, and didn't lurk behind the two-way glass. She was guaranteed some privacy with her commanding officer.

Fucking Ian. On any other day, his little stunt would have gone unnoticed. Maybe he'd have enjoyed a few more hours of freedom while the stories all got sorted. She carried bruises he put there. He wouldn't have stayed free for long.

Fate had something else in mind. His call came through only hours after Agent John Espen arrived to swing his dick around.

"This is bullshit, Crewe. There's no reason for an investigation. Why is he really here?"

"He says he was informed of your admission to the clinic and is here to follow up." Crewe scratched his eyebrow with his middle finger. "He's here now. There's nothing I can do about that."

Even though he kept a professional face, Sloan could feel the fury rolling off the man. He made the air almost unbreathable. She understood. He'd been given command of his squad and ordered to make the Supernatural Enforcement Agency palatable to the supes they aimed to police. But he and his were still second class compared to the rest of the agents. They could still be pushed around, jobs revoked, careers ended. All at the whim of assholes who hated them.

They'd been through so much and there was still no end in sight.

Sloan gritted her teeth. Unfair. It was the sort of injustice she wanted to ease and she hated she played a part in bringing attention down on Crewe and his people. "What do I need to do? August is innocent in this. I'll tell Espen I tricked him into taking me out there."

"You're going to keep your mouth shut. You're going to give up on this little side quest of yours. Keep your head down, heal up, and let this all blow over." Crewe cleared his throat. "You're not half bad, Kent. We'd hate to lose you."

Sloan swallowed back her sudden wave of emotion. The man owed her nothing. She wasn't one of his and had been tossed his way as punishment. He could have let her flounder in boredom on a desk assignment until she got frustrated enough to quit.

That she'd earned his respect and a place on his team meant the world to her.

Maybe her place was in Bearden after all.

She ignored the cut to her heart that said otherwise. One man did not make or break a place. If she survived this challenge, she could survive seeing Lorne around town.

"Let's do this," she said.

The walk down the hall and into the interrogation room where Agent John Espen waited felt like a walk to the gallows. She hoped there would be a stay in execution before the final drop.

She settled into a chair and folded her hands on the table. Crewe took the spot next to her while she studied Espen from under her lashes.

Beady eyes, pale skin. She didn't like referring to Internal Affairs agents as rats, but he did not challenge the derogatory term in the slightest. Rise to the occasion, she wanted to urge him.

Espen looked up from making a note on his pad of paper. Cold eyes met hers and she resisted the urge to shiver.

"Thank you for making time for me on such short notice, Agent Kent." He snapped his words out sharply. "Are you ready to begin?"

As if she had a choice.

Sloan dipped her chin once. "Yes."

Espen shoved a recorder between them and hit a button. "Interview with Agent Sloan Kent, accompanied by Special Agent in Charge Desmond Crewe and conducted by Agent John Espen." He clicked a pen and held it above the pad of paper. "Agent Kent, in your own words, please take me through your contact with Mr. Ian Bennett."

She began from her first introduction to the man—the briefing on the campground attack. Her words settled as she reported each subsequent step of the investigation. She didn't justify anything and stuck to the facts. Ian was spotted. He was brought in for questioning on her tip. He vandalized her home. A confrontation ended with a fight.

Facts were her friend. Embellishments or extra explanations would only derail the story she wanted to tell. She didn't want to give Espen any reason to dive down a rabbit hole.

The man jotted down a final note after she finished speaking. "Do you have a history of taking matters into your own hands, Agent Kent?"

Sloan pressed her lips together. "I do not."

"Never acted erratically?"

"No."

"Do you believe your sympathies have clouded your judgment?"

She stared at him in shock as the words registered. "I'm sorry, my what?"

Espen barely looked up from his notepad. "Your sympathies. You made accusations against a partner in the past. Perhaps you were so worried about those coming up in your new assignment that you took a tougher stance on Mr. Bennett than necessary."

"He attacked me." Pleasantries were forgotten as her voice took on a hard edge.

"Mr. Bennett maintains he acted in self-defense. He was simply trying to reconnect with an estranged relative—"

"In the middle of the night, with no announcing his presence?" Sloan scoffed. "This is ridiculous. He's just saying whatever he thinks will stick."

"Is he? This trouble began after *you* spotted him in a local drinking establishment. After *you* accused him of vandalizing your property. After *you* brandished your weapon at him. Now you've been found following him around."

She gaped at him. "What are you saying?"

"It wouldn't be the first time an agent doubled down on a problematic attitude when questioned on a call."

Sloan narrowed her eyes, suspicion building in her gut. Sympathies. Accusations. Those weren't the words of a man looking to get to the bottom of the story. His sudden appearance made more sense if he was already looking to cause trouble.

She tongued her teeth and crossed her arms over her chest. Jimmy swore to make her life miserable and make her pay. He couldn't have reached so far, could he? She knew the Agency had deep problems that she wanted to help fix, but even this seemed too much. IA helped put Jimmy away in the first place!

Dead snakes skins and stalking were child's play compared to tying her up in internal investigations and stripping her of her badge. What chance did she have of walking into another agency or police station with that black mark on her background check?

Her heart hammered against her breastbone and her palms slicked with nerves. He couldn't do this to her! He was in the wrong, not her. She'd stood up for the innocent victim and now she was being thrown to the wolves.

Sloan swallowed hard to keep herself in check. Everything she ever wanted was blowing up right before her eyes. Forced to move to Bearden, she tried to find her place. She attempted to make friends and form bonds. She wanted to make the best of the situation and set down roots. Start over.

Those roots had been slashed to pieces. Those bonds set on fire. She'd gotten her friends in trouble and didn't have anyone to vent with at home.

"Agent Kent has done nothing to make me question her judgment," Crewe rumbled next to her.

"Except for lying to her partner and allegedly becoming romantically involved with a relative of Mr. Bennett's." Espen dismissed Crewe with a flick of his eyes. "I'm here to make sure the Agency isn't given another black eye in the media. The frankly disturbing allegations Mr. Bennett has lodged against Agent Kent have escalated beyond what I was initially called in to check out. Until a full investigation into her conduct can be concluded, I'm recommending suspension."

Sloan folded her hands together and stared straight ahead. Inside, she died.

# CHAPTER 19

Head pounding, Lorne squinted at the sun. Too bright, and still too high in the sky. Too many hours to go until he could drown himself in a bottle of whiskey and keep his bear from taking his skin.

His inner animal ripped at him over the plan. Lorne locked the beast down tight and bounced along the road. Letting the bear run away with him and forcing the issue seemed like a damn good way to get shot.

He'd kept a careful balance of working himself to exhaustion and drinking away the rest of his will in the days since Sloan booted him from her room at the clinic. She didn't want to see him. She'd made it clear with the ignored calls and unanswered texts.

The unease sitting in his chest wasn't something he could push on her when she made the choice to sever their growing connection.

Better this way, he lied to himself. The sick feeling tying his stomach up in knots and buzzing around his brain was worth every second if it kept her safe. If she wasn't part of his life, then Ian and the remnants of the Bennett clan had no reason to go after her.

Lorne turned off the dirt track and onto the paved road leading away from the ranch, noting a black SUV parked along the shoulder down the road. Whatever. No skin off his back if the fuckers wanted to waste their time watching the ranch. Ian wasn't likely to show up again where they could see him.

He hated Ethan for sending him into town for supplies, but the job gave him the chance to avoid the rest of the clan. They weren't willing to let him slip into quiet observation for long without pushing —constantly pushing—for some reaction or discussion. He didn't want to talk about his feelings. Forcing the issue brought his bear out in clawing, brawling force. Those were the only moments he'd felt at peace. But blood was just a temporary balm, and he hurt worse when he forced his bear to step aside for his human half instead of letting the creature run straight for Sloan.

The SUV pulled onto the road as soon as he passed. Lorne glared at the flashing lights in his rearview. No good could come from the meeting.

Law abiding citizen he was, he slowed and came to a stop.

Only one person was inside the vehicle, as far as he could tell. August Snow, Sloan's partner, stepped out of the SUV and sauntered toward his truck with his hands casually within reach of the weapons on his waist.

Like he was the danger. Lorne wanted to bite the man.

Instead, he rolled down his window and did his best not to bare his teeth. "You following me?"

"Something like that." August rubbed a hand over his shaved head. "You talked with Sloan?"

He blinked slowly. "Not since she was hurt."

"Thought as much. So you don't know she's been suspended."

That gave him pause and forced him to reconsider driving over August's foot in his haste to get away. "She didn't do anything wrong."

"Yeah, most of us agree. She's in some shit, but she has people in her corner. In the office." August smelled uncomfortable. "Listen, man. I'm not going to tell you how to go about your business—"

"Why do I feel like that's exactly what you're about to do?" Lorne asked with a slow shake of his head.

The other man made a noise in the back of his throat and glanced away, then back again. His jaw tightened with resolve. "I've been working with her for a few weeks now—"

"You left her out in the middle of a storm."

"You telling me it's all campfire roasts and dancing around up at that ranch?" August dropped his sunglasses down his nose and glared over the frames. "Yeah, thought not. You're not police, but you understand making a place for yourself in an established clan. I regret it was a bad storm. I don't regret seeing her find the balls to tell us all to fuck ourselves. In rougher language."

No lie. A hint of respect laced his voice, too, which calmed Lorne's bear a fraction. Pride that others recognized their mate's toughness smoothed over the hard edges of his irritation.

Not his mate. Not when she rejected him.

The buzzing in his brain crackled painfully.

"She needs a partner," August continued. "And I'm not talking about when she's on duty. She needs one for all the other shit. She's your mate, isn't she?"

Lorne's bear broke through the shackles he'd placed around the beast. He closed his eyes and counted to five, trying to hold back the flood of instinct brought on by the word. "No," he growled. "She doesn't want me."

"Yeah, sure. Maybe. I'm guessing you got all protective of her and she bit your head off because she's as tough as they come. Am I close?"

Lorne grunted.

"You see where you went wrong, don't you? This woman has fought for everything. Then you come busting in and make her feel small. That's why I'm telling you she needs a partner. She needs to know you have her back, through the good decisions and the fucked up ones. You can be the protective mate without stepping on her toes."

Lorne twisted away from August and stared straight ahead. Open road, open possibilities. Only, a thick forest and jagged mountaintops blocked his view. "She's not going to make it easy."

"Oh, no. Not at all," August laughed. "I expect she'll make you crawl over glass before she even entertains the idea of mating you." August grinned. "But the scars are worth it in the end. A woman like her... I've only seen one ready to latch on as hard as she could. My Alicia."

Pride filled his scent and stabbed at Lorne. August was just one more example of what he lacked.

He seemed to be the only one who believed he couldn't have that life.

"One more thing." August reached into his pocket and drew out a slip of paper. "Your boy Ian. This is his last known address. He'd be smart to have moved on by now, but somehow I think the stubborn idiot gene runs deep in the family."

Lorne took the paper carefully. "Why are you giving me this?"

"Because if it was my family messing with my mate, nothing would stop me. As a sworn agent, I stand by the law of the land." A growl entered his voice, and he straightened. "As a shifter, I'd kill anyone who laid a hand on my mate."

## CHAPTER 20

Lorne pulled to a stop just down the road from Sloan's home. He could see the end of her Jeep between the trees. His mate was inside. If he inhaled hard enough, he could probably catch a trace of her scent.

His shoulders tightened with protective unease. If he knew she was home, who else could be watching?

Ian just wouldn't give up. Sloan, either, it seemed. Both were stubborn, but only one had good intentions in her heart.

He brought Ian's attention on her. What would have been a minor brush with the law bloomed into revenge and obsession because of his connection.

She'd be better off if he just vanished. Her tears

would dry up. She'd get her badge back. He'd find Ian and give him the end he deserved.

Lorne's fingers wouldn't budge. His bear grabbed him by the nape of the neck and shook him senseless.

She needed a partner, August said. Someone to watch over her and help her out when she was pinned down. Ethan made a similar point. She was determined to stick her foot in trouble. Only way to keep her safe was stepping in the same mess.

He'd been running for years from bonding to anyone. The last ones he made had been viciously snapped. His family, his clan, gone in an afternoon. He'd been made an outsider because he wanted to include someone in his life.

He'd kept his distance from everyone after that. Oh, he meddled and provoked to keep his world steady. But those actions weren't spotted by the others, and he still got to keep his head low.

He was seeing them in a new light, though. They were the actions of a man desperate for some connection, and scared witless that he'd lose his entire world all over again. So he lied to himself about what he wanted or why he did the things he did. He kept to the shadows. He stuck to the background.

He couldn't do that with Sloan. If he wanted her, he had to commit to everything. No slinking around. No setting her up on a pedestal to be handled gently. She needed someone on her level, be it in the muck or working to fix the world.

His brothers, his cousins, the rest of that monstrous clan, he couldn't let them wrap him up in their ghosts. He had living to do. And that started with the woman who questioned him at every turn.

Frustrated growl building in his throat, Lorne killed his engine and flung himself out of his truck. Long strides carried him to the door he beat with a fierce knock.

He heard her slowly move inside and his bear ripped him to shreds. His fault she shuffled along. Those bruises were because of him.

Sloan cracked the door open an inch. She made a pissed off hissing sound and tried to slam the door in his face.

Lorne wedged his foot in the crack to keep it open. Asshole move, probably, but he needed to have words with her. "August sent me."

Sloan stopped trying to squeeze his foot into oblivion. "He doesn't know when to keep his beak out of someone's business," she said after a loaded moment.

"Please," he murmured. "I need to talk to you."

Finally, she stepped away from the door and let him follow her inside.

Her face looked even worse than he imagined. Unholy colors still splotched her skin in angry blues and purples. Her messy hair hadn't seen a brush, and he wondered if she'd slept a wink.

Knives sliced through Lorne. His fault.

Sloan lifted her chin, blue eyes sparkling dangerously as if daring him to say anything.

He cleared his throat. "I'd be worried except for the fact that August is mated."

"Why are you here, Lorne?" she asked without any amusement in her tone.

Well, there went trying to make her laugh. He pulled his Stetson off his head and toyed with the brim. "Because I couldn't stay away."

She moved slowly back to the kitchen, holding her side like she needed to keep herself together. Lorne winced and followed closely behind. No breaks, the doctor said. Just lots of bruising and slow, human healing.

Those facts didn't make Sloan's pain any easier to stomach.

She poured herself a glass of water and leaned

against the counter. She took a sip, watching him over the rim of her glass with a blank expression.

The lack of an offer to sit or a drink didn't go unnoticed. She didn't expect him to stick around long.

Lorne needed to prove that assumption wrong.

He cleared his throat. None of the words he vaguely thought of to say seemed right. He wasn't good at this shit. There was a reason why he kept quiet most of the time. Words weren't easy. He needed time to think them over.

The blue of her eyes turned icy cold. No time to think. He was on the spot.

"We're from different people, Sloan. That doesn't make either of us right or wrong. We're both."

No response. Not even an arched eyebrow. Lorne wondered suddenly if that was how she got suspects talking. The disappointed mother routine had him stifling the urge to fidget under her stare.

And then his bear was off with sendings of her with a rounded stomach. Balls. He didn't even know if she wanted kids. He'd make a terrible father. If he had cubs, though, he hoped they'd be raised up with a strong moral compass and even stronger spine, just like Sloan.

"I want you to be safe. Always. But you shouldn't need to sacrifice any part of yourself to make me comfortable. You're going to get in dangerous spots. You're going to get cuts and scrapes. I have to accept that because those things make you the woman I can't get out of my head. Even when those dangerous spots are connected to me." His fingers tightened around the brim of his hat. "That's the give and take of this thing. There's no shutting the door on any part of our lives. You're going to be touched by my life, same as I'd be touched by yours. Warning you away from my troubles isn't how a mate should behave."

She sucked in a tiny breath. Her hand flattened against the counter as she steadied herself. "Mate?" she asked softly.

Lorne met her eyes. He wanted her to see the honesty in his. "Mate. I've been running from it the moment I first met you, thinking I was protecting you somehow. That wasn't fair to you. I took that choice from you, instead of giving it to you. So here it is. I come from a fucked up clan of bears, with at least one still surviving and trying to hurt me. I keep my distance from everyone because there's a real chance one of those fucked up bears will finish the job they started years ago. I have blood on my hands,

Sloan, and you're a good woman. You don't deserve my dirt."

She pressed her lips together and fixed him with a level look. "I've been beaten up and suspended from my job. I am *filthy* with mud."

His fault. His mud.

"What happened?"

Sloan turned back to the sink and refilled her glass. Her scent was a mix of hurt and anger. Still quiet, she shambled past him and slowly settled on the couch.

Lorne itched to follow her and pull her into his arms. He wanted to tuck her under blankets and bring her anything she needed. His bear demanded it. There was no blood to be spilled at that moment; his mate needed him.

He scratched at his beard. Her choice. She had his words. He wouldn't push her to choose him back.

His bear roared in his head.

"I'll leave if you don't want me here. I just needed you to know—"

"Stay." The word punched out from her lips.

He stepped through the kitchen, following the path she took. He took a seat at the other end of the couch, careful to give her space. "Your turn to let me in."

"I didn't want you to have a monopoly on stupid actions, so I took one for the team. I lied to August about having a doctor's appointment, and tricked him into a stakeout." She shrugged off her wry smile. "I didn't want you to find Ian first. I didn't want you to get more blood on your hands. I thought if I could bring him in, I could save you some hurt. And I was pissed at what he did to me.

"I upset a lot of people when I reported my old partner. My punishment didn't stop with my transfer here. I don't think they ever really stopped trying to fuck with me, you know? It just got harder for them. I wasn't in the same city, so they had to work to make me miserable."

"Sloan, what happened?"

"Messages, at first. Letters in the mail about how I'll get mine one of these days. Calling me Snitch Bitch like some playground bully. Snake skins because I'm a snake."

She stopped suddenly and chewed on her lower lip, looking away from him. It took every ounce of willpower to swallow back the growl and urge to track down the asshole who made her feel unsafe and unwelcome.

Lorne crawled his hand closer and squeezed hers. "What else?"

"A photo. The first time we kissed."

They'd both been watched then. Ian was after him, but someone else was after her.

Lorne fought against the instincts wanting to ball his fists and make the problem disappear. Right then, he was needed at her side. Partners worked together. One couldn't ride off into the sunset without the other.

"And now Internal Affairs is breathing down my neck, using the whole Ian bullshit as an excuse to make it look like I have a problem with shifters." Another shrug, but her scent was furious. "It's Jimmy, I know it. He just won't take responsibility for his crimes. I'm the one at fault because he couldn't accept not being at the top of the food chain."

"Why stay?" Lorne raised his hands before she could snap. After what he'd promised her, he was sure that was where she immediately jumped. "I'm not saying give up on the job. But there are other places you could work. Hell, you could probably get a job working on an enclave's police force."

Her shoulders slumped like she'd never even considered the idea. Maybe she hadn't.

"Leaving doesn't feel right. My dad, he was a cop. He always fought for good. I want to do that, too.

Changing one mind can make a difference. One correction of an injustice. The world doesn't have to be a shitty place. Giving up on fixing things feels like giving up on him. Quitting feels like letting them win." She shook her head in defiance. "Screw them. They won't break me. No matter what they try next."

"Fuck 'em." He scooted closer. Sloan stiffened when he draped an arm over her shoulder, then settled against him with a small sigh. "No matter what you choose to do, it'll work out."

"How can you say that? You can't predict the future."

Her breath was soft against his chest. Sadness filled her scent. Lorne couldn't stop his fingers stroking the silky strands of her hair. Perfect. Not the emotions. He hated for her to feel anything but happy. The sharing, however. That felt right.

He nuzzled a cheek against her hair. "Because I know you're stubborn and tough enough to kick down any door standing in your way."

Sloan pushed away from him. Blue eyes held him in place and she lifted her chin. "You know none of this is your fault, right? I don't want you here because you think it's the noble thing to do."

Lorne blinked in surprise at the sudden change in direction. "My cousin. My fault." He brought her knuckles to his lips. "But I'm here because of you. I felt like I was dying without you."

A smile ghosted her lips. "Stomach all twisted up and migraine with the force of a thousand hangovers?"

"A million." And she was the cure to them all.

"Good. Call that your penance." She watched him, serious again. "You're not responsible for someone else's actions, Lorne. What happened back then and what is happening now are on them, not you. The only thing you did was care. Someone who looks at that and decides it's wrong is the one who needs their head checked. Not. You."

His heart split wide open, so wide that he hurt to consider sewing it closed again. In the middle of her own crisis, she worried about him. Selfless woman. She was too good for him and he was too selfish to give her up.

What had the mates told her the night they all got drinks together? The world was one way, then another. He felt those words in his bones. He couldn't give up on her, just like she refused to give up when confronted with any problem in the world. She felt too perfect in his arms.

The slip of paper in his pocket burned through his jeans as he drew her back against him. Maybe he wasn't responsible for Ian's actions. He could take action anyways.

He needed to set the world right for her.

"READY?" Lorne asked quietly.

He looked at the men with him. Alex looked positively crazy, eyes wide and lips peeled back in a silent snarl. Ethan was more reserved, but just as ready for the fight. Hunter bounced on his toes, while Jesse stared straight ahead at the door with grim determination written on his face.

Fur and dominance and anger colored their collective scents. His bear rolled through him. They were clan. They were family. Together, they would keep all their mates safe.

Together.

The word echoed through his head. He was finally taking his place in the clan. No more working from the background or pretending he didn't give a shit. Ethan told him he needed to decide where he belonged. The elusive home was made clear when Sloan stepped into his life. He wanted to stand by her side and he wanted to do it with the men who were ready to throw down and fight next to him.

The Black Claw clan was his family. They accepted all the parts of him, not just the ones that meshed with their warped view of the world. Humans, shifters, it didn't matter to them. They were just trying to get by.

They wouldn't judge him for finding happiness with someone unexpected. They'd give him as much shit as any other day, then clap him on the back and wish him congratulations.

They were better than the Bennetts that raised him.

Lorne kicked open the door of the motel. Ian jerked awake, but the men streaming in with him each grabbed a limb and held him down even in his wild thrashing.

Lorne stuffed a cloth in Ian's mouth before slapping a strip of duct tape over it. Then he wound the roll around his ankles to keep him secure.

The glowing of Ian's eyes meant his bear was ready to rip through him and maul all their faces. Too bad Lorne nicked the pair of silver cuffs Sloan carried. He slapped them around Ian's wrists and watched the glow of his inner animal die.

Silently, the clan helped him carry Ian to the waiting pickup and tossed him into the bed like a sack of grain. Three hopped in the back to make sure Ian didn't buck himself over the edges.

No one said a word as they drove back toward Bearden, then blew right past the turnoff. A little further, and Lorne killed the headlights and turned the truck off the road. Empty land stretched out in front of them, as quiet as the grave.

He knew the spot he needed. The pile of dirt served as a marker under the dark and cloudless sky. He pulled to a stop and unloaded with the rest of the others.

The tailgate creaked as he unlatched it. Ian kicked and scrambled to get away from him, but there was nowhere to go. Lorne hooked a hand around his bound feet and dragged him out of the bed of the pickup. Ethan grabbed Ian's hands. Together, they tossed him into a pre-dug hole where he landed with a hard thunk.

"You never should have gone after her, Ian. You never should have tracked me down."

Ian's eyes blazed. Muffled curses were shouted around the cloth and tape. The noises grew louder and more panicked when the first shovel of dirt landed on his legs.

All four men picked up a shovel and worked to fill the hole back up. Lorne knelt at one edge and watched. The anger left his cousin's eyes. A sliver of fear replaced it.

He'd be a liar if he said it didn't stroke some dark part of himself. This was for Lilah. This was for Sloan.

Sloan's world crashed into his and his threatened to take her from him. He always worried about leaving someone behind to cry tears he didn't deserve, but he'd been wrong. Those tears meant someone gave enough of a shit to shed them. They were a sign of living a good life. He intended to keep on breathing, but that required solving one of the problems beating down his door.

That was love. The ephemeral feelings weren't enough. It was dealing with the practical matters and working at it, seeing every day to the end. Sloan deserved a better man than him, but she was just crazy enough to stick with him. He'd offer her a hand back to her feet. That was all she needed. She was tough, and he respected the hell out of her determination to keep fighting.

When the dirt was more than a light dusting, Lorne stood. The others stopped, leaning on the handles of their shovels and leering at the man in the hole.

"Last warning," Lorne growled. "Leave town

tonight. Don't ever come back here. Don't even think this place's name. I will bury you alive if I see you again. Understand?"

Ian's head bobbed up and down even before he finished speaking. The others looked silent questions at him until Lorne dipped his chin to his chest. They were done here and done with Ian.

Unless he stepped foot in Bearden again.

Not even bothering to undo Ian's bonds, they stepped back into the night. Shovels clattered into the bed of the truck and the Black Claw clan silently left the man in his potential grave.

Lorne's inner bear rumbled with satisfaction. Sloan would be pleased no blood was shed. The beast was content to keep her safe.

Lorne was happy to shut the door on a part of his life that had molded him in all the wrong ways.

The clan stayed quiet until he reached the road and flicked on the headlights.

Through the middle window pane, Hunter shouted, "Remind me never to piss you off!"

Ethan chuckled and turned up the radio.

# CHAPTER 21

By the fourth day of her suspension, Sloan was convinced there were a finite number of cat pictures a person could reasonably consume in one day. She'd hit hers before noon, and hours before she had any hope of distractions from a certain cowboy. Unlike her, *someone* had a job to get to that lasted between dawn and dusk.

Her snappy attitude wasn't Lorne's fault. He'd been nothing but supportive since barging back into her life. A little overbearing in the care department, but she expected that wasn't something she could avoid.

Truthfully, it'd been nice to have someone prop up her pillows and settle her on the couch before he left for the day and care for her when he returned at night. She wasn't bedridden and could do everything herself, but the acts melted her heart. He was there for her. After all that happened, he still showed up and had her back.

No, she was bored and had nothing to do.

Heal up. Take it easy. Those were swear words when the man who'd bruised up her ribs and face had disappeared off the face of the planet and she stared down the dark tunnel with no light at the end for her career.

The problems were of her own making, she knew that. She should have backed off when Crewe ordered her to stand down. Instead, she'd tricked August into a stakeout when she should have been on the lookout for another swift kick while she was down.

Still, something bothered her about Agent John Espen. His questions weren't right. They scratched at an itch and made her want to dig.

No one willing to talk to her had any information on the guy. The limited searches she had available as a civilian found nothing. Not surprising considering what department he worked for. The agents investigating other agents needed to keep to the shadows.

Even if he was dirty or connected to Jimmy, there

wasn't much he could do. She operated clean. No marks had been made against her. The bullshit with Ian would be cleared up and there were zero rules about who she saw when she was off duty. Espen didn't have a leg to stand on and his accusations wouldn't hold up.

She had faith in the system. She just hated that the investigation was taking so long.

Frustration bubbled out of her in a heavy groan as she studied the intricate nothingness of her ceiling. She wasn't made to sit still. She needed action.

Sloan was in a great pout about missing city life and the variety of food delivery available within fifty minutes when her phone rang. Out in the boonies of a boonie town offered few options. Barbecue, diner, a nebulous fine dining restaurant that promised to post daily specials on their social media accounts but hadn't updated those in over six months...

"Hello?" she answered.

"Sloan? Hi? This is Alicia, August's mate?"

Questions, all of them, with worried inflections on the end. Sloan jerked to attention. "Hey, Alicia. What can I do for you?"

Alicia let off a soft sigh. "I was wondering if you've heard from August? He said he was going to drop off some stuff for you after he left the office, but that was a couple hours ago."

"Not since this morning, no." Which wasn't that surprising. In their line of work, when something could pop up unexpectedly at any moment, plans changed. Her partner had mentioned earlier he had some cookies baked by his sweet mate to drop off, but he'd never reached out to confirm the time. She'd just assumed other duties needed his attention.

"I'm sure everything is okay," she reassured Alicia.

Alarm bells rang in her head, though. Maybe she was still running high from her injuries or Espen trying to fuck with her career, but something wasn't right. August wouldn't leave his mate hanging. He'd at least shoot off a text to let her know he caught something and would be late.

"I'll make some calls, if you'd like," Sloan offered.

"No, no, it's fine. I'm probably worrying about nothing. Don't bother yourself on my account," Alicia insisted.

After a few more pleasantries, Sloan ended the call and drummed her fingers against the couch. The spot between her shoulder blades itched. Something wasn't right.

She chewed on her lower lip and tried to put

herself in August's shoes. The biggest case they'd been working was Ian Bennett. Maybe something else dropped. Maybe the shifter responsible for attacking that poor family in the campground bit another victim or, hopefully, had been properly identified. Or, entirely mundane, his phone died and he hadn't noticed.

Each one of those had a rebuttal already in place. He'd been pulled from the Bennett case because of her. If anything happened in or around Bearden, she'd have heard the gossip ten times over already. August liked randomly telling Alicia a whole mess of sappy stuff and always had a phone charger nearby.

Sloan dialed Crewe. Just in case, she told herself. If nothing else, she could badger the man for updates on her own bullshit.

"Kent, was just about to ring you," Crewe barked. The background was loud with voices. "You heard from Snow?"

Sloan scooted herself to sitting and considered letting the next shifter she saw take a few nibbles just to jumpstart the healing process. "No. That's why I was calling you. Alicia wanted to know if I'd talked to him. What's going on?"

"Probably nothing. You rest up, okay? Don't worry—"

Tires crunched up her driveway. A quick glance at the clock said it was early for Lorne's arrival, but maybe the others in his clan sent him packing.

The horn beeped. She turned and winced when her ribs protested the sudden movement. Another honk had her pushing to her feet. Whatever he needed better be good.

"Crewe," Sloan snapped. Her heart jammed into her throat. "That's my partner. What's going on?"

The activity in the background faded as Crewe stepped away. "He's missing. Went out for a late lunch and hasn't shown back up. His radio is silent. Tracking on his rig puts him where he said he'd be, but that was hours ago."

She twitched aside her curtains. An older SUV, definitely not SEA-issue, parked sideways across her driveway. August sat behind the wheel, not Lorne.

The car horn honked again.

"Crewe, I'll have to call you back. August just showed up at my place."

"By the Broken," Crewe snarled. "You have him report in. Immediately."

Sloan hung up on the string of curses and orders. She had her own questions. Why he wouldn't get out of the damn SUV and knock on her door like a polite person, for starters.

She flung open the door and stepped out onto the porch, prepared to give him an earful for worrying his mate and apparently abandoning his proper vehicle for whatever janky number he'd driven to her place.

August shook his head and shouted at her through the windshield, but she couldn't read his lips or hear him over the blaring horn.

A rustle of clothing was her warning. She jerked to the side and avoided most of the blow to the back of her neck. The glancing punch from the butt of the gun was still enough to send her stumbling down the porch steps and into her yard, phone flying from her hand.

Agent Espen.

His beady eyes tracked her movements as he took a slow step forward. "Sloan Kent. You always had a problem with partners, didn't you? They're the ones that take the fall for you."

Sloan shook her head, feeling like she'd stepped into a conversation at its end. "What are you talking about?"

"First it was Jimmy Culpepper. Poor Jimmy, locked up because his bitch of a partner had to cover up her own crimes."

"No. No, that's not what happened." Sloan took a

step toward the SUV. Now that she was closer, she could see August's hands taped down to the steering wheel. His twists and tugs pounded him against the horn.

A bullet ricocheted off the ground and made her flinch away.

Espen lowered his weapon. "Now you're here in the thick of those shifters. Can't help yourself here, either. Poor August Snow is going to see exactly what you think about those filthy animals."

"They're people just like us," she said, mind racing. Fuck. Fuck! Espen was caught up in the bullshit with Jimmy. August, now, too. He was her partner! She wouldn't...

Do to him what Jimmy did to his shifter victim.

The blood drained from her face. Whether Espen intended to let her live or not, she doubted August would make it. She had to get Espen away from her partner.

Frantically, she looked around her. She was caught between a road with no idea if anyone would pass and a murderous agent clunking down her steps. No path to a weapon, no keys to get in her own Jeep even if she had room to back out, no way to bust August loose before the danger was on her.

Sloan darted into the trees.

# CHAPTER 22

An hour or less, judging by the sun in the sky. Then he'd be done with work for the day and could get back to tending Sloan.

The urge was as powerful as ever, but he didn't feel like he'd been run over and dragged for miles. Not since she let him into her home and put up with his care. His bear was pleased with the situation. Content. The push for more was a simple flashed image away, but the beast was patient. She'd accepted the word mate and that was enough for the time being.

She was within reach. The claiming mark could wait.

His idiot bear danced through his head like a trained circus animal. Sendings pushed into Lorne's mind of the mark on Sloan's skin. He quashed the dumb grin that threatened to take over his entire face. Head under the hood of Tansey's junk car, he kept his giddiness to himself.

Only a couple more hours, then he'd have his mate back in his arms.

The rumble of vehicles flying up the road pulled him out of his thoughts and mechanical work. He straightened to see two black SUVs speeding up the dirt track, kicking clouds up as they took the turns with dangerous precision.

Ethan glanced up after letting a horse loose into the paddock. "What now?"

At the far end, Alex watched with his hand on the calf needing extra care. The attention rippled to Jesse and Hunter, too, who poked their heads out of the barn.

The vehicles slammed to a stop right in the middle of the yard. Crewe stepped out of one, followed by others. They may as well have been statues for all the emotion they showed on their faces. Their scents were another matter. Concern poured off them in buckets.

"Lorne Bennett," Crewe called. He hid his eyes behind mirrored shades, but his head turned enough to take in the entire scene.

He stepped forward, wiping his hands on a cloth from his back pocket. "What of it?"

"Need to know if you've had any communication with Sloan Kent or her partner today."

His bear roared to life and battered at the unease creeping down Lorne's spine. Too many people for a question a phone call could have answered.

"I left her this morning before coming here," he answered reluctantly. "August, a couple days ago. What's going on?"

His nostrils flared. "Nothing of concern."

"Bullshit." Lorne took a step closer, growl rattling in his throat. Of course. Crewe showed to asked the question in person to test for a lie. Lorne's shoulders prickled with unease. "What really brought you here?"

Crewe lifted the sunglasses from his face and settled them on his head. Arms crossed, he focused Lorne with a steely look. "Snow has gone silent. Kent said she had eyes on him before also going quiet."

Ian. Motherfucker. He'd been warned, and he'd gone after Sloan again. Must have been him.

Lorne's bear shoved to the surface. No more warnings. Only blood would do, now.

Crewe held up a finger as a command to wait

when his phone rang. Lorne itched at the silent order, but Ethan's sharp look kept him from jumping in his truck and speeding off while the inept assholes yakked away the day.

Crewe stalked away to take the call. Not far enough. Lorne heard every word.

"There's no one at the house. Two vehicles in the driveway, plates are being run now. Got three scents here, but no good trails, like they've been covered with something."

The wheels of his mind spun. Ian hadn't disguised himself any of the times he'd taken a swing at them. Why would he start now? Or go after Sloan's partner, too? Lorne directed a narrowed glare at Crewe's phone.

Crewe cut the call short and spun a finger in the air to round up the rest of his men. The statues packed themselves away in their SUVs without a word.

Fuck that. No thought to him, no explanation? Lorne put himself in Crewe's path and let his bear roll through him. He knew his eyes flashed and he didn't care about the growl sawing in his chest. "She's missing?" Lorne demanded.

Crewe tried to step around him, but Lorne

blocked him again. "I don't have time for this," the man rumbled.

"It's that fucking fed, Espen. Has to be." Lorne's growl kicked up a notch, his words almost inhuman. If not Ian, then the threat came from Sloan's past. He never should have left her side. He should have brought her to the ranch to keep her close. If any harm came to his mate...

His bear tore at his center. Danger. Mate. Those were words that weren't ever supposed to be together.

Crewe's eyes narrowed. "What do you know about that?"

"I know Sloan suspected he was dirty. I know she's been getting harassed since before she moved here. I know it hasn't stopped."

"Harassed? What are you talking about? My people?" His eyes blazed golden and power whipped off him hard enough to make the statues he'd brought with him shuffle.

"Not that she knows." Lorne spread his hands wide. "She's been followed. Had shit sent to her in the mail. She said it was related to the guy she put away before being sent here."

"Dirty. Rat. Bastard," Crewe ground out. He

swung his attention back to the statues. "Load up. Call every last person in. We're not letting this fucker mess with any of ours." To Lorne, he growled, "Stay."

"You think keeping a man from his mate will be any different than last time?" Lorne rolled his head and cracked his neck. The rest of the clan stepped up next to him. "You better have more men than this to restrain us. We'll be in our trucks and following right behind otherwise."

A muscle jumped along Crewe's jaw. "Fine," he said tightly. "You stay behind us and don't get in the way. I won't have you ruining this for us."

"You think I give a shit about protecting a crime scene or whatever you're worried about? Sloan is my only concern." Lorne turned his back on the man and started making his way toward his truck.

Crewe stopped him with a hand on his shoulder. "And they're both mine. Don't get in the way."

SLOAN LEANED against a thick tree trunk and tried to catch her breath. Her side felt engulfed in flames. Each breath she sucked down burned her lungs.

Over the sound of her pounding heart, she listened. To the birds in the trees, the bugs buzzing in uncaring ignorance of the troubles going on around them. Mostly, she listened for any clue of where Espen stepped.

He'd driven August into the woods with them. She'd seen the two marching with tape slapped over August's mouth and a gun pointed at his back.

She'd tried to double back to grab her phone or, hell, even get shoes on and her own weapon to take the bastard down, but he'd been too quick for her and cut her off within sight of her house.

Her only hope was to keep him on the move until someone showed up. Crewe wouldn't let her languish away after dropping the bomb that August was in her driveway. Not when the man had been missing for hours.

Someone would check. If not someone from the office, Lorne was due to visit after dark. She held to the belief like her life depended on it.

Maybe it did.

"Don't do it, Kent!" Espen shouted in mocking tones. "He's a good man!"

A gunshot rang through the woods. The sudden noise silenced the chirps of birds.

Sloan squeezed her eyes closed at August's curse of pain. Small victories. He was alive enough to growl out promises of payback.

She pressed herself against the tree trunk and willed her heart to stop racing. There wasn't any waiting if Espen was already shooting. She couldn't leave her partner to the madman.

Sloan glanced around for anything she could use as a weapon and tried to make a plan. Only sheer luck had kept her from being captured so far. She couldn't run very fast or very far with her side screaming at her to slow down.

Time to get back to nature. Maybe she should have begged harder for her parents to send her to summer camp. City kids just couldn't survive in the middle of nowhere with sticks and stones.

"Come out, you dumb bitch!" Espen yelled again.

Sloan paused the ramble of her thoughts and cast a look around her. If all she had to work with were sticks and stones, she'd sure as fuck break some bones.

She crouched down and grabbed the thickest branch near her. Silent prayers were whispered into the universe in the hopes that someone listened. No lightning bolts flashed through the sky to strike down Espen, so she was on her own. She hoped she wasn't making a mistake.

"You're running out of time, you gangrenous dickhole!" Sloan shouted.

Rustled footsteps ran in her direction, then stopped. She mouthed a curse of her own and gripped the branch tightly, feeling every bump and groove under her palms.

Espen stepped closer. Closer again.

Sloan swung the club as hard as possible, ignoring the fiery pain in her side. Muscles and bruising be damned. She had a partner to save.

Wood and skull connected with a sickening thud that carried her forward a stumbling step. Espen went down with a groan.

She toed at him with her bare foot. His head rolled to the side with like a puppet cut from its strings. A quick pat down showed nothing of value she could use to restrain him. No gun, either. Fucker must have stashed it somewhere. Balls.

Straightening, Sloan quickly retraced Espen's steps. She didn't know how long he'd stay out. She had to find August and get out of the woods. No leaving a man behind.

Her stomach dipped at the sight of August in the middle of a small clearing. His eyes were wide with shock and he kept his hands pressed to his leg as he tried to scoot through the dirt. Red dampened his pants and seeped down one ear.

Sloan jogged the rest of the way to him and knelt

at his side. "August, come on." She pulled on his arm and groaned when her side protested. At least there weren't any stitches to reopen. A little pain was survivable. "Time to shift."

"Fucker shot me full of silver." August clenched his teeth. The hand pressed to his leg seeped with blood. "I'm not going anywhere."

"Don't give me that crap. You're going to fight through this. Would Alicia want anything different?" Okay, no big, badass animal to protect them. No weapon. Just bare hands, bare feet, and a man losing more blood than she was comfortable seeing.

*Think, Sloan. Think.*

She could tie something around his leg to slow the flow of blood. Find a big stick to use as a crutch and help him hobble back to her cabin. They could hole up once inside and wait for backup to track the fucker and lock him up.

August jerked his attention over her shoulder and she knew they were caught.

Sloan rose to her knees and raised her hands. Each step Espen took to stand in front of her sounded like a death knell.

She lifted her chin and met his beady eyes. She would not die at the hands of a rat-faced asshole filled with more hate than good sense. She wouldn't drag August down with her, either. They both had too much to live for.

Lorne's face flashed through her mind. She refused to let the memory of him be the last contact they had.

"Let us go," she said flatly.

"Neither of you are going anywhere," Espen answered with a smirk.

"Think about this, John." His name tasted like ashes. She used it anyway. If she could get through to the humane side of him, maybe she could buy them time or walk out of the woods all holding hands and agreeing to meet up for milkshakes later. She'd break bread with just about anyone if they changed their mind about murdering her. "Really think hard. You're in the middle of shifter territory. Someone will track you down and pin this on you. There's no going back to your regular work."

"You think I don't know that? This has all been arranged. Once you're out of the way, I'm off to a cozy island where I'll sip drinks out of coconuts and fuck the natives till I'm dead."

Gross, but okay. That spoke volumes. Fuck him, and Jimmy, and all the other assholes in the Agency who wanted a pure, human world. Change happened. If their tiny little dicks couldn't deal, they were the problem. Not her, and definitely not August.

"Supposed to be a quick, in and out. Jimmy wanted you brought as low as you pushed him. What better way than to see you take the fall for the same shit he did? You with your fucking bleeding heart for these animals."

Espen gestured at August with a dangerous lack of trigger discipline. Sloan resisted the urge to jerk to the side and cover him from every possible angle. The sharp movement was more likely to set Espen off than prevent more injuries.

"Maybe I should just let him maul you. Give him a fighting chance. You'd like that, wouldn't you, animal?" Espen tossed a gun between them. He jerked his chin at Sloan. "Pick it up. Fitting, you killing him with his own service weapon."

She shook her head hard enough to rattle. "Just think for a minute," she pleaded again.

Espen fired a round into the ground near August's leg. "I said pick it up!"

Fuck. Shit. Damn.

Hands shaking, Sloan inched forward and wrapped her fingers around the weapon.

"You point that at me, your friend will have his

BREAKING FATE

brains splattered in an instant." Espen took a step closer to August and lined up his shot.

"Going off script, aren't you?" New tactic. Appealing to his sense of good didn't work. "Jimmy never liked it when I didn't listen to him exactly."

True. Red flags were planted over every inch of the man's body. She was certain the victim she saw wasn't his first. He was still searching for more, even while he served out his prison sentence.

Espen narrowed his eyes. "Fight, or I find every single person you care about and bleed them slowly before they die." His lips lifted in another smirk like he relished the idea. "You, Snitch Bitch, there's that whole ranch. You fucking them all, or just the mopey one?"

The smirk filled Sloan with fury. Hurt her, fine. She pissed off the wrong people. Drag an innocent man into the mess? She'd do her best to make sure he never saw the outside of a cell again.

"And you, animal. Your animal kids and animal wife have enough in 'em to paint a whole fuckin' house."

August snapped his eyes to Espen and snarled.

All the moments of her life piled up. The good, the bad, and all the grays in the middle. She'd tried to live by a code. Everyone deserved a chance until they didn't, and even after they blew it, they had ways to balance the scales. Justice existed for everyone. She'd devoted herself to the idea.

Would her father have been proud?

Would Lorne?

Her heart cracked open at the thought of the man. They were so close to jumping into something big. He'd changed her world, mucked it up and made it better all at once.

Unfair. Unfair that she'd been pushed to Bearden in the first place. Unfair that it was being ripped away from her when she wanted to make it her home.

Sloan shook her head again. "No. No, I won't do it. Kill me yourself. I won't play your dirty games."

"You do it. Do it right now! You kill him, and you pay like Jimmy. He kills you, you pay and we show the world how fucking dangerous these abominations really are. Do it!"

August canted his head slightly. His eyes jerked to the side and away from Espen.

Sloan stilled and tried to listen over the man's continued ranting. It was a struggle; the sounds were almost too quiet to hear. But she trusted August's enhanced senses. If he tried to signal something to her, it was there.

Finally, just as Espen seemed to wind down into more orders to put on his own personal fucked up fight club, she heard it. Rustles of clothing and cracks of branches underfoot.

Glowing eyes surrounded them.

She never knew such relief as seeing a pack of wild animals running amongst humans armed to the teeth. The order for silence ended as soon as they were spotted, growls and snarls filling up the woods.

"No!" Espen yelled. He fired into the oncoming rush over his shoulder as he tried to run.

Sloan took careful aim and fired the gun he'd given to her to shoot August.

Espen toppled to the ground with a harsh scream and groped at the new hole in his ass.

Sloan sagged, gun falling from her hands. Then strong arms wrapped around her. Lorne. The mix of earthy cologne and manly scent filled her nose as the shock of the entire ordeal coursed through her body in wave after wave of uncontrolled shaking.

Lorne cradled her close to his chest. She wrapped her arms around his neck and clung to him as hard as she could manage.

August, supported by Crewe, hobbled to Espen and kicked him hard in the side. "No one threatens my family," he snarled and let loose another savage kick.

Sloan turned her face and pressed closer to Lorne. "You came," she mumbled against his neck.

"Of course I did. I couldn't let you get in trouble by yourself." He cupped the back of her head and stroked a hand over her hair. "Tough Sloan. Such a fighter."

She huffed a laugh. "I don't feel like much of one. I just... ran. Ran and hid and did what I could to save August."

"Sometimes surviving is all you can do." He stroked a hand down her hair again. Amusement colored his voice when he spoke again. "And sometimes you can shoot the fuckers in the ass and make them pay for kicking you down."

"Kent!" Crewe shouted from across the clearing. August still leaned against him. "No sneaking off until I get your report!"

Sloan clung to Lorne for a second more. He came for her. No rebuke for getting in trouble on his lips, just simple support as soon as he had her in his arms. That was the care she wanted from a partner. He had her back.

Life had a way of changing in the blink of an eye. She never expected to find her partner drawing blood or to be shunted aside for standing up for what was right. One moment changed her life forever and pushed her down a path she never imagined for herself, and now couldn't imagine changing.

The jittery shakes disappeared by the time she let Lorne help her to her feet. "Right away, sir."

And then home. With Lorne.

# CHAPTER 23

H ours of questions and answers and more questions left Sloan exhausted by the time Lorne finally killed the engine of his truck in front of his little house on Black Claw Ranch.

Lights twinkled in at least one window of every home, no doubt waiting for them to return and give a full accounting of her ordeal. Sloan wanted nothing to do with more questions, and everything to do with the man holding her hand like he couldn't bring himself to let her go.

He'd been quiet through it all. Not even a growl rattled in his chest as she was taken into back rooms, then told to wait, taken again, then ordered to keep waiting. Something was bursting inside the man, but he'd kept it all contained while around her squad.

She appreciated that. Maybe it was because of the mate bonds and the instinctive natures of their inner animals, but the shifters were more acquainted and patient with the protective concern of their homes. They didn't talk shit about worrying husbands and wives the same way humans did. Still, Lorne held his tongue and waited for that part of her day to end before he loomed large in the other part of her life.

Sloan held her breath as he helped her out of his truck and they made their way into his home. She didn't know what to expect from him. She had her hopes, after their last big talk, but he was facing the realities of her job once more.

Lorne leaned against the doorframe, arms crossed over his chest. "I was worried today," he said, voice rough.

He watched her with hungry eyes, the gaze of a man who'd accepted every part of her and wasn't running.

"Of what?"

"I didn't want you hurt."

Heat whipped through Sloan's body under his scrutiny. Too hot. Much too hot.

She peeled off the top she'd taken from her locker at the SEA field office, leaving her in the dirty tank top of the ordeal. August's blood still stained the hem. She held back most of her wince, but that was enough to drag Lorne's attention from her face and down her body.

"I can take care of myself," she said defensively.

"Didn't say I doubted you," he shot back, taking a step towards her.

Gold churned in the eyes he raised to her face and Sloan inhaled sharply. She held his gaze; no desire to look away existed. She was as caught in his look as she'd been caught in danger that afternoon. The edges of her vision darkened as her focus tunneled in on her shifter.

Hers.

Her chest rose, her nostrils flaring as his scent surrounded her, almost as if she had his better senses. Earthy, rich, slightly sharp scent of a male always just a little on edge.

Lorne had an unhappy past that left him a little wild and rough around the edges. That hint of unpredictability and danger didn't frighten her. She wanted to lash herself to him.

"And now?" Sheer force of will kept her voice steady. She needed his answer like it was air and food. The next words out of his mouth would be ones that determined her future. She would live or die by them.

Sloan leaned back, fingers gripping the edge of the table. His hands settled on either side of hers as his body leaned her backward, the small of her back curving, head lolling to the side as his mouth nuzzled her collarbone and a shiver rolled through her.

"Now," he replied in a whisper, "I'm just afraid of not living my entire life with you. I'm afraid of not living up to your standards."

"My standards? I have none, according to former Agent John Espen."

Lorne snorted. "I'm sure Agent August Snow would vehemently disagree."

Her breath caught with his slight growl, and released when his teeth nipped at her neck. She'd have a nice blemish there come morning, but it was only a superficial mark.

Not a claiming bite. Not yet.

"You amazed me today, Sloan." Lorne's arms wrapped around her waist as he hoisted her gently onto the table. "I don't doubt that you'll keep amazing me. Forever."

The word sounded like a vow, and a warning. She let go of the table, let go of any lingering doubts, and buried her hands in his hair.

Rough man. Protective man. Her man. Her bear.

"Is that a promise?"

The gold of his eyes brightened. "Do you want it to be?"

"After today? After everything?" Her lips twitched in a smile. "Damn straight."

A moment of stillness washed over them. He studied her, she watched him.

A heartbeat.

Another.

She was certain, as certain as she would ever be about anything. Punishment brought her to Bearden, but Lorne made her want to stay. She'd been challenged right alongside him, she saw how small she was in the overwhelming shittiness of revenge and payback, but she still made a difference.

She couldn't have done it without Lorne, or his clan, or her new squad. Each one offered her a lesson on letting others guard her back. They gave her strength to keep trying to make the world a better place, one righted wrong at a time.

Lorne had been the last face to roll through her mind when she thought hers over. Her stomach ached at the remembered sense of loss. If there was ever a lesson learned in a wild chase through the woods by an enemy sent to frame her up for murder, it was to hold those dear to her heart close.

"You already told me I was your mate. I want to make it fact."

"I'm no good for you."

"You were there when I needed you. As much as you pretend not to care for others, you have a streak of caring a mile wide."

"And an unsavory past."

"Who doesn't have to fend off murderous relatives and ex-coworkers?" Sloan shrugged off the hurt. "We match. We're fighters. They didn't change us for the worse. That's what counts."

Pride lit up his eyes. "You never lose an opportunity to make the world better, do you? I think I love your optimism the most." His palms skimmed up her sides, barely touching her. "You're still hurt," he said carefully.

Sloan swallowed hard. Her heart thundered in her chest. "So be gentle."

His strength, the speed with which he snatched her off the table and into his arms, still stunned her. The hallway was a blur as Lorne killed the steps between them and his bedroom. Theirs, now, maybe. Details to worry about in the morning.

After the weeks, the evening they'd had, she was still on edge. She wanted to pace and fight. Maybe she was more like a shifter than human in that regard. Her blood was up. The energy needed to go somewhere.

The wood floor didn't creak under the predatory grace of his stride. Inside the bedroom, he lowered her to the bed, the worn cotton of the comforter soft under her skin. Here, in his den, his scent filled her nose. It smelled like life and laughter and a future that wouldn't slip through her fingers.

Sloan hooked her legs around his waist and pulled him down on top of her, mattress dipping under their weight.

Lorne rested his arms on either side of her head, lowering his mouth to sip at her lips. She nipped at him, biting down and burying her fingers in his dark hair. Anchoring him to her, inhaling his breath as the kiss deepened, their tongues tangling together in an intimate dance.

They'd been so close to losing each other. Her fingers tightened in his hair, her kiss growing more desperate. She didn't want to waste any time. She wanted him.

Forever.

Strong hands wrapped around her wrists and pressed her arms into the bed above her head. Lorne glanced up quickly, checking to see if she showed any signs of pain, and Sloan melted. Even in the midst of everything, she was his first concern. He had her back, always.

Forever.

She bucked, hips grinding against him. "I'm fine," she insisted. Panted, even. Her skin felt on fire, his every touch raising the temperature a thousand degrees more. She'd combust soon if he didn't give her more than the rolling of his hips against hers and the attention of his mouth.

"Of course you are." He transferred her wrists to one hand and dipped his face to her shoulder, leaving a trail of biting kisses to her earlobe. "Tough Sloan. Sexy Sloan."

A shiver worked down her spine. Hot breath and scratchy beard felt so good against her skin. Too good. Almost as good as the fingers Lorne delved under her top. Fabric bunched and inched up until she lifted slightly. He tugged her shirt off just enough to twist around her wrists and keep her captive for an extra second.

"Lorne," she huffed.

"Had to find a way to keep you gentle," he insisted with a laugh.

Her retort died when he pulled down the cups of her bra and took a stiff nipple between his lips. She tossed her head back, eyes closing, and melted into his touch.

She wiggled her hands out from the shirt trap and trailed them over his head, shoulders, anywhere she could reach. "Need to feel your skin."

Lorne inhaled, gaze as bright as the stars in the sky, his lips hitching up in a sexy, indulgent, promising smirk that said she may have said the words, but he only acted because he wanted to. That silky smooth confidence of a man who knew he was in charge dried her throat.

He reared back, rising to his feet to shed his clothing in jerky movements. Sloan wet her lower lip, taking in every square inch of his hard, toned body. Packed muscles were defined by deep lines, solid chest, tapered waist.

Hers.

Desire coursed through her at the sight, even more at the obvious signs saying he wanted her as much as she did him. She doubted she'd ever wake again and not find the man attractive. He hit every mark on a checklist designed specifically for her. Tall, dark, broody, good.

She could feel red brushing over her cheeks and down her body. She slammed her thighs closed to ease some of the tension, and drew the eyes of her beast.

"No," he said, voice hoarse. "Off."

The order vibrated through her and her hands moved to obey, only to be knocked aside by his. All teasing had disappeared from his expression, leaving only dominance and a slightly animalistic need.

He rolled her jeans down her thighs, taking her panties with them. She kicked the clothes off her legs as he knelt at the foot of the bed.

"Mine," he growled.

Again, the witty words she tried to push past her lips died the moment he touched her. He licked a long line up her slit, then lapped at her clit, breath hot on her flesh.

Lorne's hands caressed her body, stroking over her hips, her stomach, kneading her breasts. Fire trailed under his hands, and his mouth worked her into oblivion. Air exploded from her lungs when he pushed a finger inside her.

Soon her entire body writhed beneath him, his flicking motions bringing her to a peak of pleasure. Her fingers curled into his scalp, digging in as he licked and stroked. A throbbing pulse beat between her legs. Ready to explode. She teetered right on the edge as he thrust another finger inside her, swirling and swiping until, until—

Her moan morphed into a cry. Lorne held her open, refusing to let her back away from the pleasure he built inside her, licking and tasting until her aftershocks rolled over into another release barreling down upon her.

"Mine," he declared again.

All she could do was nod and suck down breath after breath. Pain ceased to exist. She'd been taken to another plane of existence, one where she and Lorne were the only inhabitants. All the better, because she didn't intend to let anything come between them again. Pasts be damned. She wanted their future. She wanted him.

He rose up, pressing tiny, soft kisses and sharp, not so tiny bites onto her skin along the way. He avoided the mass of bruises still on her ribs, growling when he nuzzled against them for a brief second, then laid another blistering kiss on her lips.

Lorne settled between her thighs, the head of his cock pressing against her. Yes, yes, *now*.

"Sloan?" he whispered against her lips.

The last, final question. His voice was hoarse with holding back, she could hear, but he still gave her the chance to change her mind.

Gentle bear. Crazy bear. She'd made her choice.

"Lorne, now," she groaned.

With a growl, he thrust into her.

Sloan cried out. He filled her, stretching her, surging past the point of gentle and into that of pure pleasure. Her body scrambled to adjust, to keep up with the intense bear. Her nails dug into his shoulders, her legs wrapped around his waist.

He was a bear, a beast. Devouring her one atom at a time, inflaming every nerve ending until even her hair crackled with wild energy.

"Yours!"

*His.*

And she wanted him. Madwoman. Crazy, crazy, crazy. Tying herself to him, with all his problems. But there she was, spread out for him, offering herself up to him, whimpering her need in his ears.

He would take care of her. Now, tonight. And forever. That was what a good mate, a good partner, did. He swore his promises to her body. He'd make the same ones with words later, if she wanted. She would have everything.

Gentle. Gentle. He tried to keep steady, slow. The

bruises along her side and the ones still coloring her face weren't as awful as when his cousin put them there, but they were still a reminder of how fragile the human in his bed could be.

Sloan was having none of that. Hard nails dragged down his back, and she set her teeth against his skin.

A high moan left her lips as she arched into his thrusts. Trembling hands trailed up and down his back, his arms, wherever she could reach. He reveled in the touch, not just as his soon-to-be mate, but as her being *there*.

Too close. He'd come too close to losing her. He hated the feeling that boiled in his stomach. Even more, he hated the idea of stripping that power away from her and urging her into something safer, something that guaranteed her home every night. She wasn't made for cages. She was made to slam through walls and terrible ideas and transform the world into a place he'd be proud to bring cubs into.

Lorne dragged himself back until only the tip remained in her heat, then slammed home again. And again. The bed rocked under the force, headboard pounding against the wall at the top of each blow.

He grabbed her hands and stretched her out

underneath him, fingers twining together as a proxy for their connection. He stared into her big blue eyes, utterly captured in the moment. Flesh slapped against flesh, her moans punctuated his groans, her body pulsed and clutched at him with every slide and slam of his hips.

His.

Perfect woman. Tough woman. His.

Running headlong into danger put her in his path. Refusing to back down kept her in his way. He wouldn't change anything about her.

At the precipice of another shattering orgasm, Lorne lowered his head to the upper swell of her breast. His gums ached with the press of fangs; his bear roared to complete the connection. Their bond would serve them both, tie them together, forge their lives onto a path they walked together.

"Mine," she whispered, nipped at his skin, too.

By the Broken, he nearly came undone right then and there.

His fangs pierced her skin, delicate beads of blood touching his tongue. He licked the scarlet liquid and tasted the salty moisture with a groan. Light flared behind his eyelids as the bond took hold in his head and heart.

His.

Warmth flooded through him, filling her. Lorne lifted his head and roared, dark tips of claws digging into the blankets by her head.

Peace flowed over him. Not the kind that came from a contented afternoon, or a long shower, or a quickie with someone he'd never see again. No, the peace that took hold was the lasting kind. The kind that soothed the rough parts of his soul and filled the cold spaces of his heart.

She'd taken him, damage and all, and made him into a complete person.

"Mine," she whispered against his shoulder.

Lorne rolled off her, gently tugging her over his chest. He never wanted to let her go. "If anything had happened to you…"

She kissed his shoulder. "Nothing did."

"Nothing ever will." His bear surged inside him, thickening his voice. "You're mine now, Sloan. Forever."

She grabbed his face between her hands and pecked him on the lips. "Forever."

"This is what you do for fun?" Sloan took a sip of her wine and squinted at the glossy polish on her nails. Serviceable and not against any uniform regulation, they didn't look half bad. The gloss was nothing like the neon green on Tansey's fingers or the navy on Joss's.

"Whenever we can manage," Joss answered between handfuls of popcorn. "It's nice to just be normal for a few hours."

Normal. What a word. She used to have a definition for it, but the time since supes entered the world changed the meaning. So she changed her definition, and again found the word turned on its head when she witnessed someone who should have upheld the law doing unspeakable things. Once again, she was forced to shift her idea of normal when she found herself in Bearden and surrounded by the Black Claw clan.

Normal, now, meant brawling shifters and the background moos and neighs of the ranch. Her new normal was actually protecting and serving the supernatural population, instead of standing by while others trumped up charges or put their own will above all else. With her place on the shifter squad restored and Agent John Espen behind bars, Sloan aimed to correct as many wrongs as she could for the rest of her life.

Absently, she traced the upper edge of the mark Lorne left on her skin. Her skin prickled at the touch and the memory of how she felt when Lorne traced the scar. Hot. Needy. It was like an on switch. Dangerous, that mark. And incredible.

Just like her mate.

That last was the best bit of the new normal.

The word still felt unfamiliar when she said it, but the meaning behind it never changed. Her mate was love and support. Lorne wrapped her up in strong arms when she needed, and helped her to her feet when she needed that, too. He had her back, and was her partner through it all. Murderous relatives and revenge-seeking assholes couldn't break them apart.

They found their place, together.

The front door burst open with loud guffaws. Ethan stormed inside. Hunter and Lorne took up flanking positions on either side.

"Get 'em," Ethan ordered.

With roars and laughter, the three men rushed into the room. Canisters appeared in their hands and sprayed white fluff. The couch took the first hit.

"Interlopers!" Tansey shouted. She snapped to her feet and tried to grab the canister from Ethan. He simply shoved her back onto the couch and into a mess.

"Raiders!" Hunter corrected with a grin, circling the couch with Joss on the other side.

Joss stepped to one side, then another, Hunter mirroring the movements. With a wild squeal, she climbed over the back and threw herself at him, riding him to the ground with a thump.

"You ruined mani and movie night!" Joss yelled, fighting to get a hold on the canister Hunter kept from her.

"We made it better!" Hunter defended and squirted her with white.

Sloan eyed the last man. Her mate stalked around

the struggles of the others, fingers twitching on the plastic top of his can.

"You're losing your touch, Agent," he said, menace in his voice contrasting with the teasing smirk on his lips.

She cast around for anything to use against him or throw him off balance. Her cohorts were useless, Joss still wrestling with Hunter and Tansey throwing back handfuls of goop at Ethan. The movie kept on playing, utterly forgotten in the chaos. "We'll have armed guards posted outside next time."

"You think we don't have a plan for that?"

Lorne slid a look over her shoulder and Sloan cursed. At both doors, Jesse and Alex stood guard, also holding canisters of their own. Both had drawn dark lines under their eyes like they'd prepared for war.

Sloan wasn't helpless. She dove toward the wrestling couple on the floor and grabbed up Hunter's can with a yell. Lorne looped his arms around her waist, but it was too late. She turned the can upside down and covered his head with the sweetness.

"Tansey! The popcorn!" she laughed.

Tansey dodged Ethan and tripped over her own feet, spilling the bowl of popcorn over Hunter and

Joss. Pieces settled into the whipped topping and gave them the look of pocked snowmen.

The room erupted into madness as the other men joined in the fight. Cans were thrown and dropped, changed sides, and emptied while the mates defended themselves against the greater numbers.

When the laughter finally died down, the mess was everywhere. Grins touched every face.

"Is that whipped cream?" Joss asked in the quiet of heaving breaths.

Hunter dragged a finger through a glob on Joss's shoulder, then stuck it in his mouth. "Mhm. You can't expect us to waste our shaving cream."

"But you'll waste whipped cream." A clump fell from Tansey's ear to the floor with a quiet splat.

"Be glad it wasn't canned cheese."

"Ethan Ashford, you are responsible for cleaning this mess up. You want to act like some drunk frat boy, you get to clean like a sober one." Oh, she tried her damnedest to sound like a harsh taskmistress, but laugh didn't quite stay out of her voice.

Ethan tackled her to the couch. She screeched and slapped away his hands, but he pinned hers under his knees. Devilish grin on his face, he squirted some into his mouth, then leaned forward to give her a sloppy kiss.

"And I'm out before this gets even weirder," Alex grumbled.

Tansey picked a piece of popcorn off her arm and threw it at him. "Not so fast. You're on cleaning duty, too. Just following orders isn't an excuse."

Crazy clan. The night was just what she needed after the weeks of trouble. Sloan felt the strain of work melt away with every full-bellied laugh.

"Hey." Lorne caught her chin between his fingers and tilted her face to his.

"Hey, yourself," she echoed. Her cheeks hurt from her smile.

Only human in the SEA shifter unit. Only true human in the clan.

Sloan was right where she belonged.

# ABOUT THE AUTHOR

Cecilia Lane grew up in a what most call paradise, but she insists is humid hell. She escaped the heat with weekly journeys to the library, where she learned the basics of slaying dragons, magical abilities, and grand adventures.

When it became apparent she wouldn't be able to travel the high seas with princes or party with rock star vampires, Cecilia hunkered down to create her own worlds filled with sexy people in complicated situations. She now writes with the support of her own sexy man and many interruptions from her goofy dog.

*Connect with Cecilia online!*
www.cecilialane.com

ALSO BY CECILIA LANE

**Shifting Destinies: Black Claw Ranch**

Wrangled Fate

Spurred Fate

Breaking Fate

Wild Fate

**Shifting Destinies: Shifters of Bear's Den**

Forbidden Mate

Dangerous Mate

Hunted Mate

Runaway Mate

Stolen Mate

Untamed Mate

**Shifting Destinies Standalone Stories**

Her Christmas Wolf

Claiming the Wolf Princess

Wanted by the Bear